AF797961

THE PROBLEMS OF PHILOSOPHY

THE PROBLEMS OF PHILOSOPHY

BY

BERTRAND RUSSELL

M.A., F.R.S.

LECTURER AND LATE FELLOW OF TRINITY COLLEGE.
CAMBRIDGE.

©Author

All rights reserved. No part of this work may be reproduced, stored, adapted, or transmitted in any form or by any means, electronic, mechanical, photocopying, micro-filming recording or otherwise, or translated in any language, without the prior written permission of the copyright owner and the publisher. The book is sold subject to the condition that it shall not, by way of trade or otherwise, be lent, resold, hired out, or otherwise circulated without the prior publisher's written consent in any form of binding or cover other than that in which it is published.

The views and opinions expressed in this book are author(s) own and the facts reported by them have been verified to the extent possible, and the publishers are not in any way liable for the same.

ISBN: 978-93-5128-613-4

First Published in1912
Indian Reprint in 2017

Published by

Kalpaz Publications
C-30, Satyawati Nagar,
Delhi – 110052
E-mail: kalpaz@hotmail.com
Website: kalpazpublications.com
Ph.: +91-9212142040

Cataloging in Publication Data—DK
Courtesy: D.K. Agencies (P) Ltd. <docinfo@dkagencies.com>

Russell, Bertrand, 1872-1970, **author.**
The problems of philosophy / by Bertrand Russell.
pages cm
"First published in 1912"—Title page verso.
ISBN 9789351286134

1. Philosophy—Introductions. 2. Metaphysics. 3. Knowledge, Theory of. I. Title.

B1649.R93P76 2017 DDC 110 23

PREFACE

In the following pages, I have confined myself in the main to those problems of philosophy in regard to which I thought it possible to say something positive and constructive, since merely negative criticism seemed out of place. For this reason, theory of knowledge occupies a larger space than metaphysics in the present volume, and some topics much discussed by philosophers are treated very briefly, if at all.

I have derived valuable assistance from unpublished writings of Mr. G. E. Moore and Mr. J. M. Keynes: from the former, as regards the relations of sense-data to physical objects, and from the latter as regards probability and induction. I have also profited greatly by the criticisms and suggestions of Professor Gilbert Murray.

CONTENTS

THE PROBLEMS OF PHILOSOPHY

CHAPTER I

APPEARANCE AND REALITY

Is there any knowledge in the world which is so certain that no reasonable man could doubt it? This question, which at first sight might not seem difficult, is really one of the most difficult that can be asked. When we have realised the obstacles in the way of a straightforward and confident answer, we shall be well launched on the study of philosophy—for philosophy is merely the attempt to answer such ultimate questions, not carelessly and dogmatically, as we do in ordinary life and even in the sciences, but critically, after exploring all that makes such questions puzzling, and after realising all the vagueness and confusion that underlie our ordinary ideas.

In daily life, we assume as certain many things which, on a closer scrutiny, are found to be so full of apparent contradictions that only a great amount of thought enables us to know what it is that we really may believe. In the search for certainty, it is natural to begin with our present experiences, and in some sense, no doubt, knowledge is to be derived from them. But any statement as to what it is that our immediate experiences make us know is very likely to be wrong. It seems to me that I am now sitting in a chair, at a table of a certain shape, on which I see sheets of paper with writing or print. By turning my head I see out of the window buildings and clouds and the sun. I believe that the sun is about ninety-three million miles from the earth; that it is a hot globe many times bigger than the earth; that, owing to the earth's rotation, it rises every morning, and will continue to do so for an indefinite time in the future. I believe that, if any other normal person comes into my room, he will see the same chairs and tables and books and papers as I see, and that the table which I see is the same as the table which I feel pressing against my arm. All this seems to be so evident as to be hardly worth stating, except in answer to a man who doubts whether I know anything. Yet all this may be reasonably doubted, and all of it requires much careful discussion before we can be sure that we have stated it in a form that is wholly true.

To make our difficulties plain, let us concentrate attention on the table. To the eye it is oblong, brown and shiny, to the touch it is smooth and cool and hard; when I tap it, it gives out a wooden sound. Any one else who sees and feels and hears the table will agree with this description, so that it might seem as if no difficulty would arise; but as soon as we try to be more precise our troubles begin. Although I believe that the table is "really" of the same colour all over, the parts that reflect the light look much brighter than the other parts, and some parts look white because of reflected light. I know that, if I move, the parts that reflect the light will be different, so that the apparent distribution of colours on the table will change. It follows that if several people are looking at the table at the same moment, no two of them will see exactly the same distribution of colours, because no two can see it from exactly the same point of view, and any change in the point of view makes some change in the way the light is reflected.

For most practical purposes these differences are unimportant, but to the painter they are all-important: the painter has to unlearn the habit of thinking that things seem to have the colour which common sense says they "really" have, and to learn the habit of seeing things as they appear. Here we have already the beginning of one of the distinctions that cause most trouble in philosophy—the distinction between "appearance" and "reality," between what things seem to be and what they are. The painter wants to know what things seem to be, the practical man and the philosopher want to know what they are; but the philosopher's wish to know this is stronger than the practical man's, and is more troubled by knowledge as to the difficulties of answering the question.

To return to the table. It is evident from what we have found, that there is no colour which pre-eminently appears to be *the* colour of the table, or even of any one particular part of the table—it appears to be of different colours from different points of view, and there is no reason for regarding some of these as more really its colour than others. And we know that even from a given point of view the colour will seem different by artificial light, or to a colour-blind man, or to a man wearing blue spectacles, while in the dark there will be no colour at all, though to touch and hearing the table will be unchanged. Thus colour is not something which is inherent in the table, but something depending upon the table and the spectator and the way the light falls on the table. When, in ordinary life, we speak of *the* colour of the table, we only mean the sort of colour which it will seem to have to a normal spectator from an ordinary point of view under usual conditions of light. But the other colours which appear under other conditions have just as good a right to be considered real; and therefore, to avoid favouritism, we are compelled to deny that, in itself, the table has any one particular colour.

The same thing applies to the texture. With the naked eye one can see the grain, but otherwise the table looks smooth and even. If we looked at it through a microscope, we should see roughnesses and hills and valleys, and all sorts of differences that are imperceptible to the naked eye. Which of these is the "real" table? We are naturally tempted to say that what we see through the microscope is more real, but that in turn would be changed by a still more powerful microscope. If, then, we cannot trust what we see with the naked eye, why should we trust what we see through a microscope? Thus, again, the confidence in our senses with which we began deserts us.

The *shape* of the table is no better. We are all in the habit of judging as to the "real" shapes of things, and we do this so unreflectingly that we come to think we actually see the real shapes. But, in fact, as we all have to learn if we try to draw, a given thing looks different in shape from every different point of view. If our table is "really" rectangular, it will look, from almost all points of view, as if it had two acute angles and two obtuse angles. If opposite sides are parallel, they will look as if they converged to a point away from the spectator; if they are of equal length, they will look as if the nearer side were longer. All these things are not commonly noticed in looking at a table, because experience has taught us to construct the "real" shape from the apparent shape, and the "real" shape is what interests us as practical men. But the "real" shape is not what we see; it is something inferred from what we see. And what we see is constantly changing in shape as we move about the room; so that here again the senses seem not to give us the truth about the table itself, but only about the appearance of the table.

Similar difficulties arise when we consider the sense of touch. It is true that the table always gives us a sensation of hardness, and we feel that it resists pressure. But the sensation we obtain depends upon how hard we press the table and also upon what part of the body we press with; thus the various sensations due to various pressures or various parts of the body cannot be supposed to reveal *directly* any definite property of the table, but at most to be *signs* of some property which perhaps *causes* all the sensations, but is not actually apparent in any of them. And the same applies still more obviously to the sounds which can be elicited by rapping the table.

Thus it becomes evident that the real table, if there is one, is not the same as what we immediately experience by sight or touch or hearing. The real table, if there is one, is not *immediately* known to us at all, but must be an inference from what is immediately known. Hence, two very difficult questions at once arise; namely, (1) Is there a real table at all? (2) If so, what sort of object can it be?

It will help us in considering these questions to have a few simple terms of which the meaning is definite and clear. Let us give the name of "sense-data" to the things that are immediately known in sensation: such things as colours, sounds, smells, hardnesses, roughnesses, and so on. We shall give the name "sensation" to the experience of being immediately aware of these things. Thus, whenever we see a colour, we have a sensation *of* the colour, but the colour itself is a sense-datum, not a sensation. The colour is that *of* which we are immediately aware, and the awareness itself is the sensation. It is plain that if we are to know anything about the table, it must be by means of the sense-data—brown colour, oblong shape, smoothness, etc.—which we associate with the table; but for the reasons which have been given, we cannot say that the table *is* the sense-data, or even that the sense-data are directly properties of the table. Thus a problem arises as to the relation of the sense-data to the real table, supposing there is such a thing.

The real table, if it exists, we will call a "physical object." Thus we have to consider the relation of sense-data to physical objects. The collection of all physical objects is called "matter." Thus our two questions may be re-stated as follows: (1) Is there any such thing as matter? (2) If so, what is its nature?

The philosopher who first brought prominently forward the reasons for regarding the immediate objects of our senses as not existing independently of us was Bishop Berkeley (1685–1753). His *Three Dialogues between Hylas and Philonous, in Opposition to Sceptics and Atheists*, undertake to prove that there is no such thing as matter at all, and that the world consists of nothing but minds and their ideas. Hylas has hitherto believed in matter, but he is no match for Philonous, who mercilessly drives him into contradictions and paradoxes, and makes his own denial of matter seem, in the end, as if it were almost common sense. The arguments employed are of very different value: some are important and sound, others are confused or quibbling. But Berkeley retains the merit of having shown that the existence of matter is capable of being denied without absurdity, and that if there are any things that exist independently of us they cannot be the immediate objects of our sensations.

There are two different questions involved when we ask whether matter exists, and it is important to keep them clear. We commonly mean by "matter" something which is opposed to "mind," something which we think of as occupying space and as radically incapable of any sort of thought or consciousness. It is chiefly in this sense that Berkeley denies matter; that is to say, he does not deny that the sense-data which we commonly take as signs of the existence of the table are really signs of the existence of *something* independent of us, but he does deny that this something is non-mental, that it is neither mind nor ideas entertained by some mind. He admits that there must be something which continues to exist when we go out of the room or shut our eyes, and that what we call seeing the table does really give us reason for believing in something which persists even when we are not seeing it. But he thinks that this something cannot be radically different in nature from what we see, and cannot be independent of seeing altogether, though it must be independent of *our* seeing. He is thus led to regard the "real" table as an idea in the mind of God. Such an idea has the required permanence and independence of ourselves, without being—as matter would otherwise be—something quite unknowable, in the sense that we can only infer it, and can never be directly and immediately aware of it.

Other philosophers since Berkeley have also held that, although the table does not depend for its existence upon being seen by me, it does depend upon being seen (or otherwise apprehended in sensation) by *some* mind—not necessarily the mind of God, but more often the whole collective mind of the universe. This they hold, as Berkeley does, chiefly because they think there can be nothing real—or at any rate nothing known to be real—except minds and their thoughts and feelings. We might state the argument by which they support their view in some such way as this: "Whatever can be thought of is an idea in the mind of the person thinking of it; therefore nothing can be thought of except ideas in minds; therefore anything else is inconceivable, and what is inconceivable cannot exist."

Such an argument, in my opinion, is fallacious; and of course those who advance it do not put it so shortly or so crudely. But whether valid or not, the argument has been very widely advanced in one form or another; and very many philosophers, perhaps a majority, have held that there is nothing real except minds and their ideas. Such philosophers are called "idealists." When they come to explaining matter, they either say, like Berkeley, that matter is really nothing but a collection of ideas, or they say, like Leibniz (1646–1716), that what appears as matter is really a collection of more or less rudimentary minds.

But these philosophers, though they deny matter as opposed to mind, nevertheless, in another sense, admit matter. It will be remembered that we asked two questions; namely, (1) Is there a real table at all? (2) If so, what sort of object can it be? Now both Berkeley and Leibniz admit that there is a real table, but Berkeley says it is certain ideas in the mind of God, and Leibniz says it is a colony of souls. Thus both of them answer our first question in the affirmative, and only diverge from the views of ordinary mortals in their answer to our second question. In fact, almost all philosophers seem to be agreed that there is a real table: they almost all agree that, however much our sense-data—colour, shape, smoothness, etc.—may depend upon us, yet their occurrence is a sign of something existing independently of us, something differing, perhaps, completely from our sense-data, and yet to be regarded as causing those sense-data whenever we are in a suitable relation to the real table.

Now obviously this point in which the philosophers are agreed—the view that there *is* a real table, whatever its nature may be —is vitally important, and it will be worth while to consider what reasons there are for accepting this view before we go on to the further question as to the nature of the real table. Our next chapter, therefore, will be concerned with the reasons for supposing that there is a real table at all.

Before we go farther it will be well to consider for a moment what it is that we have discovered so far. It has appeared that, if we take any common object of the sort that is supposed to be known by the senses, what the senses *immediately* tell us is not the truth about the object as it is apart from us, but only the truth about certain sense-data which, so far as we can see, depend upon the relations between us and the object. Thus what we directly see and feel is merely "appearance," which we believe to be a sign of some "reality" behind. But if the reality is not what appears, have we any means of knowing whether there is any reality at all? And if so, have we any means of finding out what it is like?

Such questions are bewildering, and it is difficult to know that even the strangest hypotheses may not be true. Thus our familiar table, which has roused but the slightest thoughts in us hitherto, has become a problem full of surprising possibilities. The one thing we know about it is that it is not what it seems. Beyond this modest result, so far, we have the most complete liberty of conjecture. Leibniz tells us it is a community of souls; Berkeley tells us it is an idea in the mind of God; sober science, scarcely less wonderful, tells us it is a vast collection of electric charges in violent motion.

Among these surprising possibilities, doubt suggests that perhaps there is no table at all. Philosophy, if it cannot *answer* so many questions as we could wish, has at least the power of *asking* questions which increase the interest of the world, and show the strangeness and wonder lying just below the surface even in the commonest things of daily life.

CHAPTER II

THE EXISTENCE OF MATTER

In this chapter we have to ask ourselves whether, in any sense at all, there is such a thing as matter. Is there a table which has a certain intrinsic nature, and continues to exist when I am not looking, or is the table merely a product of my imagination, a dream-table in a very prolonged dream? This question is of the greatest importance. For if we cannot be sure of the independent existence of objects, we cannot be sure of the independent existence of other people's bodies, and therefore still less of other people's minds, since we have no grounds for believing in their minds except such as are derived from observing their bodies. Thus if we cannot be sure of the independent existence of objects, we shall be left alone in a desert—it may be that the whole outer world is nothing but a dream, and that we alone exist. This is an uncomfortable possibility; but although it cannot be strictly *proved* to be false, there is not the slightest reason to suppose that it is true. In this chapter we have to see why this is the case.

Before we embark upon doubtful matters, let us try to find some more or less fixed point from which to start. Although we are doubting the physical existence of the table, we are not doubting the existence of the sense-data which made us think there was a table; we are not doubting that, while we look, a certain colour and shape appear to us, and while we press, a certain sensation of hardness is experienced by us. All this, which is psychological, we are not calling in question. In fact, whatever else may be doubtful, some at least of our immediate experiences seem absolutely certain.

Descartes (1596–1650), the founder of modern philosophy, invented a method which may still be used with profit—the method of systematic doubt. He determined that he would believe nothing which he did not see quite clearly and distinctly to be true. Whatever he could bring himself to doubt, he would doubt, until he saw reason for not doubting it. By applying this method he gradually became convinced that the only existence of which he could be *quite* certain was his own. He imagined a deceitful demon, who presented unreal things to his senses in a perpetual phantasmagoria; it might be very improbable that such a demon existed, but still it was possible, and therefore doubt concerning things perceived by the senses was possible.

But doubt concerning his own existence was not possible, for if he did not exist, no demon could deceive him. If he doubted, he must exist; if he had any experiences whatever, he must exist. Thus his own existence was an absolute certainty to him. "I think, therefore I am," he said (*Cogito, ergo sum*); and on the basis of this certainty he set to work to build up again the world of knowledge which his doubt had laid in ruins. By inventing the method of doubt, and by showing that subjective things are the most certain, Descartes performed a great service to philosophy, and one which makes him still useful to all students of the subject.

But some care is needed in using Descartes' argument. "*I* think, therefore *I* am" says rather more than is strictly certain. It might seem as though we were quite sure of being the same person to-day as we were yesterday, and this is no doubt true in some sense. But the real Self is as hard to arrive at as the real table, and does not seem to have that absolute, convincing certainty that belongs to particular experiences. When I look at my table and see a certain brown colour, what is quite certain at once is not "*I* am seeing a brown colour," but rather, "a brown colour is being seen." This of course involves something (or somebody) which (or who) sees the brown colour; but it does not of itself involve that more or less permanent person whom we call "I." So far as immediate certainty goes, it might be that the something which sees the brown colour is quite momentary, and not the same as the something which has some different experience the next moment.

Thus it is our particular thoughts and feelings that have primitive certainty. And this applies to dreams and hallucinations as well as to normal perceptions: when we dream or see a ghost, we certainly do have the sensations we think we have, but for various reasons it is held that no physical object corresponds to these sensations. Thus the certainty of our knowledge of our own experiences does not have to be limited in any way to allow for exceptional cases. Here, therefore, we have, for what it is worth, a solid basis from which to begin our pursuit of knowledge.

The problem we have to consider is this: Granted that we are certain of our own sense-data, have we any reason for regarding them as signs of the existence of something else, which we can call the physical object? When we have enumerated all the sense-data which we should naturally regard as connected with the table, have we said all there is to say about the table, or is there still something else—something not a sense-datum, something which persists when we go out of the room? Common sense unhesitatingly answers that there is. What can be bought and sold and pushed about and have a cloth laid on it, and so on, cannot be a *mere* collection of sense-data. If the cloth completely hides the table, we shall derive no sense-data from the table, and therefore, if the table were merely sense-data, it would have ceased to exist, and the cloth would be suspended in empty air, resting, by a miracle, in the place where the table formerly was. This seems plainly absurd; but whoever wishes to become a philosopher must learn not to be frightened by absurdities.

One great reason why it is felt that we must secure a physical object in addition to the sense-data, is that we want the *same* object for different people. When ten people are sitting round a dinner-table, it seems preposterous to maintain that they are not seeing the same tablecloth, the same knives and forks and spoons and glasses. But the sense-data are private to each separate person; what is immediately present to the sight of one is not immediately present to the sight of another: they all see things from slightly different points of view, and therefore see them slightly differently. Thus, if there are to be public neutral objects, which can be in some sense known to many different people, there must be something over and above the private and particular sense-data which appear to various people. What reason, then, have we for believing that there are such public neutral objects?

The first answer that naturally occurs to one is that, although different people may see the table slightly differently, still they all see more or less similar things when they look at the table, and the variations in what they see follow the laws of perspective and reflection of light, so that it is easy to arrive at a permanent object underlying all the different people's sense-data. I bought my table from the former occupant of my room; I could not buy *his* sense-data, which died when he went away, but I could and did buy the confident expectation of more or less similar sense-data. Thus it is the fact that different people have similar sense-data, and that one person in a given place at different times has similar sense-data, which makes us suppose that over and above the sense-data there is a permanent public object which underlies or causes the sense-data of various people and various times.

Now in so far as the above considerations depend upon supposing that there are other people besides ourselves, they beg the very question at issue. Other people are represented to me by certain sense-data, such as the sight of them or the sound of their voices, and if I had no reason to believe that there were physical objects independent of my sense-data, I should have no reason to believe that other people exist except as part of my dream. Thus, when we are trying to show that there must be objects independent of our own sense-data, we cannot appeal to the testimony of other people, since this testimony itself consists of sense-data, and does not reveal other people's experiences unless our own sense-data are signs of things existing independently of us. We must therefore, if possible, find, in our own purely private experiences, characteristics which show, or tend to show, that there are in the world things other than ourselves and our private experiences.

In one sense it must be admitted that we can never *prove* the existence of things other than ourselves and our experiences. No logical absurdity results from the hypothesis that the world consists of myself and my thoughts and feelings and sensations, and that everything else is mere fancy. In dreams a very complicated world may seem to be present, and yet on waking we find it was a delusion; that is to say, we find that the sense-data in the dream do not appear to have corresponded with such physical objects as we should naturally infer from our sense-data. (It is true that, when the physical world is assumed, it is possible to find physical causes for the sense-data in dreams: a door banging, for instance, may cause us to dream of a naval engagement. But although, in this case, there is a physical *cause* for the sense-data, there is not a physical object *corresponding* to the sense-data in the way in which an actual naval battle would correspond.) There is no logical impossibility in the supposition that the whole of life is a dream, in which we ourselves create all the objects that come before us. But although this is not logically impossible, there is no reason whatever to suppose that it is true; and it is, in fact, a less simple hypothesis, viewed as a means of accounting for the facts of our own life, than the common-sense hypothesis that there really are objects independent of us, whose action on us causes our sensations.

The way in which simplicity comes in from supposing that there really are physical objects is easily seen. If the cat appears at one moment in one part of the room, and at another in another part, it is natural to suppose that it has moved from the one to the other, passing over a series of intermediate positions. But if it is merely a set of sense-data, it cannot have ever been in any place where I did not see it; thus we shall have to suppose that it did not exist at all while I was not looking, but suddenly sprang into being in a new place. If the cat exists whether I see it or not, we can understand from our own experience how it gets hungry between one meal and the next; but if it does not exist when I am not seeing it, it seems odd that appetite should grow during non-existence as fast as during existence. And if the cat consists only of sense-data, it cannot be *hungry*, since no hunger but my own can be a sense-datum to me. Thus the behaviour of the sense-data which represent the cat to me, though it seems quite natural when regarded as an expression of hunger, becomes utterly inexplicable when regarded as mere movements and changes of patches of colour, which are as incapable of hunger as a triangle is of playing football.

But the difficulty in the case of the cat is nothing compared to the difficulty in the case of human beings. When human beings speak —that is, when we hear certain noises which we associate with ideas, and simultaneously see certain motions of lips and expressions of face—it is very difficult to suppose that what we hear is not the expression of a thought, as we know it would be if we emitted the same sounds. Of course similar things happen in dreams, where we are mistaken as to the existence of other people. But dreams are more or less suggested by what we call waking life, and are capable of being more or less accounted for on scientific principles if we assume that there really is a physical world. Thus every principle of simplicity urges us to adopt the natural view, that there really are objects other than our selves and our sense-data which have an existence not dependent upon our perceiving them.

Of course it is not by argument that we originally come by our belief in an independent external world. We find this belief ready in ourselves as soon as we begin to reflect: it is what may be called an *instinctive* belief.

We should never have been led to question this belief but for the fact that, at any rate in the case of sight, it seems as if the sense-datum itself were instinctively believed to be the independent object, whereas argument shows that the object cannot be identical with the sense-datum. This discovery, however—which is not at all paradoxical in the case of taste and smell and sound, and only slightly so in the case of touch—leaves undiminished our instinctive belief that there *are* objects *corresponding* to our sense-data. Since this belief does not lead to any difficulties, but on the contrary tends to simplify and systematise our account of our experiences, there seems no good reason for rejecting it. We may therefore admit—though with a slight doubt derived from dreams—that the external world does really exist, and is not wholly dependent for its existence upon our continuing to perceive it.

The argument which has led us to this conclusion is doubtless less strong than we could wish, but it is typical of many philosophical arguments, and it is therefore worth while to consider briefly its general character and validity. All knowledge, we find, must be built up upon our instinctive beliefs, and if these are rejected, nothing is left. But among our instinctive beliefs some are much stronger than others, while many have, by habit and association, become entangled with other beliefs, not really instinctive, but falsely supposed to be part of what is believed instinctively.

Philosophy should show us the hierarchy of our instinctive beliefs, beginning with those we hold most strongly, and presenting each as much isolated and as free from irrelevant additions as possible. It should take care to show that, in the form in which they are finally set forth, our instinctive beliefs do not clash, but form a harmonious system. There can never be any reason for rejecting one instinctive belief except that it clashes with others; thus, if they are found to harmonise, the whole system becomes worthy of acceptance.

It is of course *possible* that all or any of our beliefs may be mistaken, and therefore all ought to be held with at least some slight element of doubt. But we cannot have *reason* to reject a belief except on the ground of some other belief. Hence, by organising our instinctive beliefs and their consequences, by considering which among them it is most possible, if necessary, to modify or abandon, we can arrive, on the basis of accepting as our sole data what we instinctively believe, at an orderly systematic organisation of our knowledge, in which, though the *possibility* of error remains, its likelihood is diminished by the interrelation of the parts and by the critical scrutiny which has preceded acquiescence.

This function, at least, philosophy can perform. Most philosophers, rightly or wrongly, believe that philosophy can do much more than this—that it can give us knowledge, not otherwise attainable, concerning the universe as a whole, and concerning the nature of ultimate reality. Whether this be the case or not, the more modest function we have spoken of can certainly be performed by philosophy, and certainly suffices, for those who have once begun to doubt the adequacy of common sense, to justify the arduous and difficult labours that philosophical problems involve.

CHAPTER III

THE NATURE OF MATTER

In the preceding chapter we agreed, though without being able to find demonstrative reasons, that it is rational to believe that our sense-data—for example, those which we regard as associated with my table—are really signs of the existence of something independent of us and our perceptions. That is to say, over and above the sensations of colour, hardness, noise, and so on, which make up the appearance of the table to me, I assume that there is something else, *of* which these things are appearances. The colour ceases to exist if I shut my eyes, the sensation of hardness ceases to exist if I remove my arm from contact with the table, the sound ceases to exist if I cease to rap the table with my knuckles.

But I do not believe that when all these things cease the table ceases. On the contrary, I believe that it is because the table exists continuously that all these sense-data will reappear when I open my eyes, replace my arm, and begin again to rap with my knuckles. The question we have to consider in this chapter is: What is the nature of this real table, which persists independently of my perception of it?

To this question physical science gives an answer, somewhat incomplete it is true, and in part still very hypothetical, but yet deserving of respect so far as it goes. Physical science, more or less unconsciously, has drifted into the view that all natural phenomena ought to be reduced to motions. Light and heat and sound are all due to wave-motions, which travel from the body emitting them to the person who sees light or feels heat or hears sound. That which has the wave-motion is either æther or "gross matter," but in either case is what the philosopher would call matter. The only properties which science assigns to it are position in space, and the power of motion according to the laws of motion. Science does not deny that it *may* have other properties; but if so, such other properties are not useful to the man of science, and in no way assist him in explaining the phenomena.

It is sometimes said that "light *is* a form of wave-motion," but this is misleading, for the light which we immediately see, which we know directly by means of our senses, is *not* a form of wave-motion, but something quite different — something which we all know if we are not blind, though we cannot describe it so as to convey our knowledge to a man who is blind. A wave-motion, on the contrary, could quite well be described to a blind man, since he can acquire a knowledge of space by the sense of touch; and he can experience a wave-motion by a sea voyage almost as well as we can. But this, which a blind man can understand, is not what we mean by *light*: we mean by *light* just that which a blind man can never understand,

and which we can never describe to him.

Now this something, which all of us who are not blind know, is not, according to science, really to be found in the outer world: it is something caused by the action of certain waves upon the eyes and nerves and brain of the person who sees the light. When it is said that light *is* waves, what is really meant is that waves are the physical cause of our sensations of light. But light itself, the thing which seeing people experience and blind people do not, is not supposed by science to form any part of the world that is independent of us and our senses. And very similar remarks would apply to other kinds of sensations.

It is not only colours and sounds and so on that are absent from the scientific world of matter, but also *space* as we get it through sight or touch. It is essential to science that its matter should be in *a* space, but the space in which it is cannot be exactly the space we see or feel. To begin with, space as we see it is not the same as space as we get it by the sense of touch; it is only by experience in infancy that we learn how to touch things we see, or how to get a sight of things which we feel touching us. But the space of science is neutral as between touch and sight; thus it cannot be either the space of touch or the space of sight.

Again, different people see the same object as of different shapes, according to their point of view. A circular coin, for example, though we should always *judge* it to be circular, will *look* oval unless we are straight in front of it. When we judge that it *is* circular, we are judging that it has a real shape which is not its apparent shape, but belongs to it intrinsically apart from its appearance. But this real shape, which is what concerns science, must be in a real space, not the same as anybody's *apparent* space. The real space is public, the apparent space is private to the percipient. In different people's *private* spaces the same object seems to have different shapes; thus the real space, in which it has its real shape, must be different from the private spaces. The space of science, therefore, though *connected* with the spaces we see and feel, is not identical with them, and the manner of its connection requires investigation.

We agreed provisionally that physical objects cannot be quite like our sense-data, but may be regarded as *causing* our sensations. These physical objects are in the space of science, which we may call "physical" space. It is important to notice that, if our sensations are to be caused by physical objects, there must be a physical space containing these objects and our sense-organs and nerves and brain. We get a sensation of touch from an object when we are in contact with it; that is to say, when some part of our body occupies a place in physical space quite close to the space occupied by the object. We see an object (roughly speaking) when no opaque body is between the object and our eyes in physical space. Similarly, we only hear or smell or taste an object when we are sufficiently near to it, or when it touches the tongue, or has some suitable position in physical space relatively to our body. We cannot begin to state what different sensations we shall derive from a given object under different circumstances unless we regard the object and our body as both in one physical space, for it is mainly the relative positions of the object and our body that determine what sensations we shall derive from the object.

Now our sense-data are situated in our private spaces, either the space of sight or the space of touch or such vaguer spaces as other senses may give us. If, as science and common sense assume, there is one public all-embracing physical space in which physical objects are, the relative positions of physical objects in physical space must more or less correspond to the relative positions of sense-data in our private spaces. There is no difficulty in supposing this to be the case. If we see on a road one house nearer to us than another, our other senses will bear out the view that it is nearer; for example, it will be reached sooner if we walk along the road. Other people will agree that the house which looks nearer to us is nearer; the ordnance map will take the same view; and thus everything points to a spatial relation between the houses corresponding to the relation between the sense-data which we see when we look at the houses. Thus we may assume that there is a physical space in which physical objects have spatial relations corresponding to those which the corresponding sense-data have in our private spaces. It is this physical space which is dealt with in geometry and assumed in physics and astronomy.

Assuming that there is physical space, and that it does thus correspond to private spaces, what can we know about it? We can know *only* what is required in order to secure the correspondence. That is to say, we can know nothing of what it is like in itself, but we can know the sort of arrangement of physical objects which results from their spatial relations. We can know, for example, that the earth and moon and sun are in one straight line during an eclipse, though we cannot know what a physical straight line is in itself, as we know the look of a straight line in our visual space. Thus we come to know much more about the *relations* of distances in physical space than about the distances themselves; we may know that one distance is greater than another, or that it is along the same straight line as the other, but we cannot have that immediate acquaintance with physical distances that we have with distances in our private spaces, or with colours or sounds or other sense-data. We can know all those things about physical space which a man born blind might know through other people about the space of sight; but the kind of things which a man born blind could never know about the space of sight we also cannot know about physical space. We can know the properties of the relations required to preserve the correspondence with sense-data, but we cannot know the nature of the terms between which the relations hold.

With regard to time, our *feeling* of duration or of the lapse of time is notoriously an unsafe guide as to the time that has elapsed by the clock. Times when we are bored or suffering pain pass slowly, times when we are agreeably occupied pass quickly, and times when we are sleeping pass almost as if they did not exist. Thus, in so far as time is constituted by duration, there is the same necessity for distinguishing a public and a private time as there was in the case of space. But in so far as time consists in an *order* of before and after, there is no need to make such a distinction; the time-order which events seem to have is, so far as we can see, the same as the time-order which they do have. At any rate no reason can be given for supposing that the two orders are not the same. The same is usually true of space: if a regiment of men are marching along a road, the *shape* of the regiment will look different from different points of view, but the men will appear arranged in the same *order* from all points of view. Hence we regard the *order* as true also in physical space, whereas the shape is only supposed to correspond to the physical space so far as is required for the preservation of the order.

In saying that the time-order which events *seem to have* is the same as the time-order which they *really have*, it is necessary to guard against a possible misunderstanding. It must not be supposed that the various states of different physical objects have the same time-order as the sense-data which constitute the perceptions of those objects. Considered as physical objects, the thunder and lightning are simultaneous; that is to say, the lightning is simultaneous with the disturbance of the air in the place where the disturbance begins, namely, where the lightning is. But the sense-datum which we call hearing the thunder does not take place until the disturbance of the air has travelled as far as to where we are. Similarly, it takes about eight minutes for the sun's light to reach us; thus, when we see the sun we are seeing the sun of eight minutes ago. So far as our sense-data afford evidence as to the physical sun they afford evidence as to the physical sun of eight minutes ago; if the physical sun had ceased to exist within the last eight minutes, that would make no difference to the sense-data which we call "seeing the sun." This affords a fresh illustration of the necessity of distinguishing between sense-data and physical objects.

What we have found as regards space is much the same as what we find in relation to the correspondence of the sense-data with their physical counterparts. If one object looks blue and another red, we may reasonably presume that there is some corresponding difference between the physical objects; if two objects both look blue, we may presume a corresponding similarity. But we cannot hope to be acquainted directly with the quality in the physical object which makes it look blue or red. Science tells us that this quality is a certain sort of wave-motion, and this sounds familiar, because we think of wave-motions in the space we see. But the wave-motions must really be in physical space, with which we have no direct acquaintance; thus the real wave-motions have not that familiarity which we might have supposed them to have. And what holds for colours is closely similar to what holds for other sense-data. Thus we find that, although the *relations* of physical objects have all sorts of knowable properties, derived from their correspondence with the relations of sense-data, the physical objects themselves remain unknown in their intrinsic nature, so far at least as can be discovered by means of the senses. The question remains whether there is any other method of discovering the intrinsic nature of physical objects.

The most natural, though not ultimately the most defensible, hypothesis to adopt in the first instance, at any rate as regards visual sense-data, would be that, though physical objects cannot, for the reasons we have been considering, be *exactly* like sense-data, yet they may be more or less like. According to this view, physical objects will, for example, really have colours, and we might, by good luck, see an object as of the colour it really is. The colour which an object seems to have at any given moment will in general be very similar, though not quite the same, from many different points of view; we might thus suppose the "real" colour to be a sort of medium colour, intermediate between the various shades which appear from the different points of view.

Such a theory is perhaps not capable of being definitely refuted, but it can be shown to be groundless. To begin with, it is plain that the colour we see depends only upon the nature of the light-waves that strike the eye, and is therefore modified by the medium intervening between us and the object, as well as by the manner in which light is reflected from the object in the direction of the eye. The intervening air alters colours unless it is perfectly clear, and any strong reflection will alter them completely. Thus the colour we see is a result of the ray as it reaches the eye, and not simply a property of the object from which the ray comes. Hence, also, provided certain waves reach the eye, we shall see a certain colour, whether the object from which the waves start has any colour or not. Thus it is quite gratuitous to suppose that physical objects have colours, and therefore there is no justification for making such a supposition. Exactly similar arguments will apply to other sense-data.

It remains to ask whether there are any general philosophical arguments enabling us to say that, if matter is real, it *must* be of such and such a nature. As explained above, very many philosophers, perhaps most, have held that whatever is real must be in some sense mental, or at any rate that whatever we can know anything about must be in some sense mental. Such philosophers are called "idealists." Idealists tell us that what appears as matter is really something mental; namely, either (as Leibniz held) more or less rudimentary minds, or (as Berkeley contended) ideas in the minds which, as we should commonly say, "perceive" the matter. Thus idealists deny the existence of matter as something intrinsically different from mind, though they do not deny that our sense-data are signs of something which exists independently of our private sensations. In the following chapter we shall consider briefly the reasons—in my opinion fallacious—which idealists advance in favour of their theory.

CHAPTER IV

IDEALISM

The word "idealism" is used by different philosophers in somewhat different senses. We shall understand by it the doctrine that whatever exists, or at any rate whatever can be known to exist, must be in some sense mental. This doctrine, which is very widely held among philosophers, has several forms, and is advocated on several different grounds. The doctrine is so widely held, and so interesting in itself, that even the briefest survey of philosophy must give some account of it.

Those who are unaccustomed to philosophical speculation may be inclined to dismiss such a doctrine as obviously absurd. There is no doubt that common sense regards tables and chairs and the sun and moon and material objects generally as something radically different from minds and the contents of minds, and as having an existence which might continue if minds ceased. We think of matter as having existed long before there were any minds, and it is hard to think of it as a mere product of mental activity. But whether true or false, idealism is not to be dismissed as obviously absurd.

We have seen that, even if physical objects do have an independent existence, they must differ very widely from sense-data, and can only have a *correspondence* with sense-data, in the same sort of way in which a catalogue has a correspondence with the things catalogued. Hence common sense leaves us completely in the dark as to the true intrinsic nature of physical objects, and if there were good reason to regard them as mental, we could not legitimately reject this opinion merely because it strikes us as strange. The truth about physical objects *must* be strange. It *may* be unattainable, but if any philosopher believes that he has attained it, the fact that what he offers as the truth is strange ought not to be made a ground of objection to his opinion.

The grounds on which idealism is advocated are generally grounds derived from the theory of knowledge, that is to say, from a discussion of the conditions which things must satisfy in order that we may be able to know them. The first serious attempt to establish idealism on such grounds was that of Bishop Berkeley. He proved first, by arguments which were largely valid, that our sense-data cannot be supposed to have an existence independent of us, but must be, in part at least, "in" the mind, in the sense that their existence would not continue if there were no seeing or hearing or touching or smelling or tasting. So far, his contention was almost certainly valid, even if some of his arguments were not so. But he went on to argue that sense-data were the only things of whose existence our perceptions could assure us, and that to be known is to be "in" a mind, and therefore to be mental. Hence he concluded that nothing can ever be known except what is in some mind, and that whatever is known without being in my mind must be in some other mind.

In order to understand his argument, it is necessary to understand his use of the word "idea." He gives the name "idea" to anything which is *immediately* known, as, for example, sense-data are known. Thus a particular colour which we see is an idea; so is a voice which we hear, and so on. But the term is not wholly confined to sense-data. There will also be things remembered or imagined, for with such things also we have immediate acquaintance at the moment of remembering or imagining. All such immediate data he calls "ideas."

He then proceeds to consider common objects, such as a tree, for instance. He shows that all we know immediately when we "perceive" the tree consists of ideas in his sense of the word, and he argues that there is not the slightest ground for supposing that there is anything real about the tree except what is perceived. Its being, he says, consists in being perceived: in the Latin of the schoolmen its "*esse*" is "*percipi.*" He fully admits that the tree must continue to exist even when we shut our eyes or when no human being is near it. But this continued existence, he says, is due to the fact that God continues to perceive it; the "real" tree, which corresponds to what we called the physical object, consists of ideas in the mind of God, ideas more or less like those we have when we see the tree, but differing in the fact that they are permanent in God's mind so long as the tree continues to exist. All our perceptions, according to him, consist in a partial participation in God's perceptions, and it is because of this participation that different people see more or less the same tree. Thus apart from minds and their ideas there is nothing in the world, nor is it possible that anything else should ever be known, since whatever is known is necessarily an idea.

There are in this argument a good many fallacies which have been important in the history of philosophy, and which it will be as well to bring to light. In the first place, there is a confusion engendered by the use of the word "idea." We think of an idea as essentially something *in* somebody's mind, and thus when we are told that a tree consists entirely of ideas, it is natural to suppose that, if so, the tree must be entirely in minds. But the notion of being "in" the mind is ambiguous. We speak of bearing a person in mind, not meaning that the person is in our minds, but that a thought of him is in our minds. When a man says that some business he had to arrange went clean out of his mind, he does not mean to imply that the business itself was ever in his mind, but only that a thought of the business was formerly in his mind, but afterwards ceased to be in his mind. And so when Berkeley says that the tree must be in our minds if we can know it, all that he really has a right to say is that a thought of the tree must be in our minds. To argue that the tree itself must be in our minds is like arguing that a person whom we bear in mind is himself in our minds. This confusion may seem too gross to have been really committed by any competent philosopher, but various attendant circumstances rendered it possible. In order to see how it was possible, we must go more deeply into the question as to the nature of ideas.

Before taking up the general question of the nature of ideas, we must disentangle two entirely separate questions which arise concerning sense-data and physical objects. We saw that, for various reasons of detail, Berkeley was right in treating the sense-data which constitute our perception of the tree as more or less subjective, in the sense that they depend upon us as much as upon the tree, and would not exist if the tree were not being perceived. But this is an entirely different point from the one by which Berkeley seeks to prove that whatever can be immediately known *must* be in a mind. For this purpose arguments of detail as to the dependence of sense-data upon us are useless. It is necessary to prove, generally, that by being known, things are shown to be mental. This is what Berkeley believes himself to have done. It is this question, and not our previous question as to the difference between sense-data and the physical object, that must now concern us.

Taking the word "idea" in Berkeley's sense, there are two quite distinct things to be considered whenever an idea is before the mind. There is on the one hand the thing of which we are aware—say the colour of my table—and on the other hand the actual awareness itself, the mental act of apprehending the thing. The mental act is undoubtedly mental, but is there any reason to suppose that the thing apprehended is in any sense mental? Our previous arguments concerning the colour did not prove it to be mental; they only proved that its existence depends upon the relation of our sense organs to the physical object—in our case, the table. That is to say, they proved that a certain colour will exist, in a certain light, if a normal eye is placed at a certain point relatively to the table. They did not prove that the colour is in the mind of the percipient.

Berkeley's view, that obviously the colour *must* be in the mind, seems to depend for its plausibility upon confusing the thing apprehended with the act of apprehension. Either of these might be called an "idea"; probably either would have been called an idea by Berkeley. The act is undoubtedly in the mind; hence, when we are thinking of the act, we readily assent to the view that ideas must be in the mind. Then, forgetting that this was only true when ideas were taken as acts of apprehension, we transfer the proposition that "ideas are in the mind" to ideas in the other sense, *i.e.* to the things apprehended by our acts of apprehension. Thus, by an unconscious equivocation, we arrive at the conclusion that whatever we can apprehend must be in our minds. This seems to be the true analysis of Berkeley's argument, and the ultimate fallacy upon which it rests.

This question of the distinction between act and object in our apprehending of things is vitally important, since our whole power of acquiring knowledge is bound up with it. The faculty of being acquainted with things other than itself is the main characteristic of a mind. Acquaintance with objects essentially consists in a relation between the mind and something other than the mind; it is this that constitutes the mind's power of knowing things. If we say that the things known must be in the mind, we are either unduly limiting the mind's power of knowing, or we are uttering a mere tautology. We are uttering a mere tautology if we mean by "*in* the mind" the same as by "*before* the mind," *i.e.* if we mean merely being apprehended by the mind. But if we mean this, we shall have to admit that what, *in this sense*, is in the mind, may nevertheless be not mental. Thus when we realise the nature of knowledge, Berkeley's argument is seen to be wrong in substance as well as in form, and his grounds for supposing that "ideas"—*i.e.* the objects apprehended—must be mental, are found to have no validity whatever. Hence his grounds in favour of idealism may be dismissed. It remains to see whether there are any other grounds.

It is often said, as though it were a self-evident truism, that we cannot know that anything exists which we do not know. It is inferred that whatever can in any way be relevant to our experience must be at least capable of being known by us; whence it follows that if matter were essentially something with which we could not become acquainted, matter would be something which we could not know to exist, and which could have for us no importance whatever. It is generally also implied, for reasons which remain obscure, that what can have no importance for us cannot be real, and that therefore matter, if it is not composed of minds or of mental ideas, is impossible and a mere chimæra.

To go into this argument fully at our present stage would be impossible, since it raises points requiring a considerable preliminary discussion; but certain reasons for rejecting the argument may be noticed at once. To begin at the end: there is no reason why what cannot have any *practical* importance for us should not be real. It is true that, if *theoretical* importance is included, everything real is of *some* importance to us, since, as persons desirous of knowing the truth about the universe, we have some interest in everything that the universe contains. But if this sort of interest is included, it is not the case that matter has no importance for us, provided it exists, even if we cannot know that it exists. We can, obviously, suspect that it may exist, and wonder whether it does; hence it is connected with our desire for knowledge, and has the importance of either satisfying or thwarting this desire.

Again, it is by no means a truism, and is in fact false, that we cannot know that anything exists which we do not know. The word "know" is here used in two different senses. (1) In its first use it is applicable to the sort of knowledge which is opposed to error, the sense in which what we know is *true*, the sense which applies to our beliefs and convictions, *i.e.* to what are called *judgments*. In this sense of the word we know *that* something is the case. This sort of knowledge may be described as knowledge of *truths*. (2) In the second use of the word "know" above, the word applies to our knowledge of *things*, which we may call *acquaintance*. This is the sense in which we know sense-data. (The distinction involved is roughly that between *savoir* and *connaître* in French, or between *wissen* and *kennen* in German.)

Thus the statement which seemed like a truism becomes, when re-stated, the following: "We can never truly judge that something with which we are not acquainted exists." This is by no means a truism, but on the contrary a palpable falsehood. I have not the honour to be acquainted with the Emperor of Russia, but I truly judge that he exists. It may be said, of course, that I judge this because of other people's acquaintance with him. This, however, would be an irrelevant retort, since, if the principle were true, I could not know that any one else is acquainted with him. But further: there is no reason why I should not know of the existence of something with which *nobody* is acquainted. This point is important, and demands elucidation.

If I am acquainted with a thing which exists, my acquaintance gives me the knowledge that it exists. But it is not true that, conversely, whenever I can know that a thing of a certain sort exists, I or some one else must be acquainted with the thing. What happens, in cases where I have true judgment without acquaintance, is that the thing is known to me by *description*, and that, in virtue of some general principle, the existence of a thing answering to this description can be inferred from the existence of something with which I am acquainted. In order to understand this point fully, it will be well first to deal with the difference between knowledge by acquaintance and knowledge by description, and then to consider what knowledge of general principles, if any, has the same kind of certainty as our knowledge of the existence of our own experiences. These subjects will be dealt with in the following chapters.

CHAPTER V

KNOWLEDGE BY ACQUAINTANCE AND KNOWLEDGE BY DESCRIPTION

In the preceding chapter we saw that there are two sorts of knowledge: knowledge of things, and knowledge of truths. In this chapter we shall be concerned exclusively with knowledge of things, of which in turn we shall have to distinguish two kinds. Knowledge of things, when it is of the kind we call knowledge by *acquaintance*, is essentially simpler than any knowledge of truths, and logically independent of knowledge of truths, though it would be rash to assume that human beings ever, in fact, have acquaintance with things without at the same time knowing some truth about them. Knowledge of things by *description*, on the contrary, always involves, as we shall find in the course of the present chapter, some knowledge of truths as its source and ground. But first of all we must make clear what we mean by "acquaintance" and what we mean by "description."

We shall say that we have *acquaintance* with anything of which we are directly aware, without the intermediary of any process of inference or any knowledge of truths. Thus in the presence of my table I am acquainted with the sense-data that make up the appearance of my table—its colour, shape, hardness, smoothness, etc.; all these are things of which I am immediately conscious when I am seeing and touching my table. The particular shade of colour that I am seeing may have many things said about it—I may say that it is brown, that it is rather dark, and so on. But such statements, though they make me know truths *about* the colour, do not make me know the colour itself any better than I did before: so far as concerns knowledge of the colour itself, as opposed to knowledge of truths about it, I know the colour perfectly and completely when I see it, and no further knowledge of it itself is even theoretically possible. Thus the sense-data which make up the appearance of my table are things with which I have acquaintance, things immediately known to me just as they are.

My knowledge of the table as a physical object, on the contrary, is not direct knowledge. Such as it is, it is obtained through acquaintance with the sense-data that make up the appearance of the table. We have seen that it is possible, without absurdity, to doubt whether there is a table at all, whereas it is not possible to doubt the sense-data. My knowledge of the table is of the kind which we shall call "knowledge by description." The table is "the physical object which causes such-and-such sense-data." This *describes* the table by means of the sense-data. In order to know anything at all about the table, we must know truths connecting it with things with which we have acquaintance: we must know that "such-and-such sense-data are caused by a physical object." There is no state of mind in which we are directly aware of the table; all our knowledge of the table is really knowledge of *truths*, and the actual thing which is the table is not, strictly speaking, known to us at all. We know a description, and we know that there is just one object to which this description applies, though the object itself is not directly known to us. In such a case, we say that our knowledge of the object is knowledge by description.

All our knowledge, both knowledge of things and knowledge of truths, rests upon acquaintance as its foundation. It is therefore important to consider what kinds of things there are with which we have acquaintance.

Sense-data, as we have already seen, are among the things with which we are acquainted; in fact, they supply the most obvious and striking example of knowledge by acquaintance. But if they were the sole example, our knowledge would be very much more restricted than it is. We should only know what is now present to our senses: we could not know anything about the past—not even that there was a past—nor could we know any truths about our sense-data, for all knowledge of truths, as we shall show, demands acquaintance with things which are of an essentially different character from sense-data, the things which are sometimes called "abstract ideas," but which we shall call "universals." We have therefore to consider acquaintance with other things besides sense-data if we are to obtain any tolerably adequate analysis of our knowledge.

The first extension beyond sense-data to be considered is acquaintance by *memory*. It is obvious that we often remember what we have seen or heard or had otherwise present to our senses, and that in such cases we are still immediately aware of what we remember, in spite of the fact that it appears as past and not as present. This immediate knowledge by memory is the source of all our knowledge concerning the past: without it, there could be no knowledge of the past by inference, since we should never know that there was anything past to be inferred.

The next extension to be considered is acquaintance by *introspection*. We are not only aware of things, but we are often aware of being aware of them. When I see the sun, I am often aware of my seeing the sun; thus "my seeing the sun" is an object with which I have acquaintance. When I desire food, I may be aware of my desire for food; thus "my desiring food" is an object with which I am acquainted. Similarly we may be aware of our feeling pleasure or pain, and generally of the events which happen in our minds. This kind of acquaintance, which may be called self-consciousness, is the source of all our knowledge of mental things. It is obvious that it is only what goes on in our own minds that can be thus known immediately. What goes on in the minds of others is known to us through our perception of their bodies, that is, through the sense-data in us which are associated with their bodies. But for our acquaintance with the contents of our own minds, we should be unable to imagine the minds of others, and therefore we could never arrive at the knowledge that they have minds. It seems natural to suppose that self-consciousness is one of the things that distinguish men from animals: animals, we may suppose, though they have acquaintance with sense-data, never become aware of this acquaintance, and thus never know of their own existence. I do not mean that they *doubt* whether they exist, but that they have never become conscious of the fact that they have sensations and feelings, nor therefore of the fact that they, the subjects of their sensations and feelings, exist.

We have spoken of acquaintance with the contents of our minds as *self*-consciousness, but it is not, of course, consciousness of our *self*: it is consciousness of particular thoughts and feelings. The question whether we are also acquainted with our bare selves, as opposed to particular thoughts and feelings, is a very difficult one, upon which it would be rash to speak positively. When we try to look into ourselves we always seem to come upon some particular thought or feeling, and not upon the "I" which has the thought or feeling. Nevertheless there are some reasons for thinking that we are acquainted with the "I," though the acquaintance is hard to disentangle from other things. To make clear what sort of reason there is, let us consider for a moment what our acquaintance with particular thoughts really involves.

When I am acquainted with "my seeing the sun," it seems plain that I am acquainted with two different things in relation to each other. On the one hand there is the sense-datum which represents the sun to me, on the other hand there is that which sees this sense-datum. All acquaintance, such as my acquaintance with the sense-datum which represents the sun, seems obviously a relation between the person acquainted and the object with which the person is acquainted. When a case of acquaintance is one with which I can be acquainted (as I am acquainted with my acquaintance with the sense-datum representing the sun), it is plain that the person acquainted is myself. Thus, when I am acquainted with my seeing the sun, the whole fact with which I am acquainted is "Self-acquainted-with-sense-datum."

Further, we know the truth "I am acquainted with this sense-datum." It is hard to see how we could know this truth, or even understand what is meant by it, unless we were acquainted with something which we call "I." It does not seem necessary to suppose that we are acquainted with a more or less permanent person, the same to-day as yesterday, but it does seem as though we must be acquainted with that thing, whatever its nature, which sees the sun and has acquaintance with sense-data. Thus, in some sense it would seem we must be acquainted with our Selves as opposed to our particular experiences. But the question is difficult, and complicated arguments can be adduced on either side. Hence, although acquaintance with ourselves seems *probably* to occur, it is not wise to assert that it undoubtedly does occur.

We may therefore sum up as follows what has been said concerning acquaintance with things that exist. We have acquaintance in sensation with the data of the outer senses, and in introspection with the data of what may be called the inner sense—thoughts, feelings, desires, etc.; we have acquaintance in memory with things which have been data either of the outer senses or of the inner sense. Further, it is probable, though not certain, that we have acquaintance with Self, as that which is aware of things or has desires towards things.

In addition to our acquaintance with particular existing things, we also have acquaintance with what we shall call *universals*, that is to say, general ideas, such as *whiteness*, *diversity*, *brotherhood*, and so on. Every complete sentence must contain at least one word which stands for a universal, since all verbs have a meaning which is universal. We shall return to universals later on, in Chapter IX; for the present, it is only necessary to guard against the supposition that whatever we can be acquainted with must be something particular and existent. Awareness of universals is called *conceiving*, and a universal of which we are aware is called a *concept*.

It will be seen that among the objects with which we are acquainted are not included physical objects (as opposed to sense-data), nor other people's minds. These things are known to us by what I call "knowledge by description," which we must now consider.

By a " description " I mean any phrase of the form " a so-and-so " or " the so-and-so." A phrase of the form " a so-and-so " I shall call an " ambiguous " description ; a phrase of the form " the so-and-so " (in the singular) I shall call a " definite " description. Thus " a man " is an ambiguous description, and " the man with the iron mask " is a definite description. There are various problems connected with ambiguous descriptions, but I pass them by, since they do not directly concern the matter we are discussing, which is the nature of our knowledge concerning objects in cases where we know that there is an object answering to a definite description, though we are not *acquainted* with any such object. This is a matter which is concerned exclusively with *definite* descriptions. I shall therefore, in the sequel, speak simply of " descriptions " when I mean " definite descriptions." Thus a description will mean any phrase of the form " the so-and-so " in the singular.

We shall say that an object is " known by description " when we know that it is " *the* so-and-so," *i.e.* when we know that there is one object, and no more, having a certain property; and it will generally be implied that we do not have knowledge of the same object by acquaintance. We know that the man with the iron mask existed, and many propositions are known about him; but we do not know who he was. We know that the candidate who gets the most votes will be elected, and in this case we are very likely also acquainted (in the only sense in which one can be acquainted with some one else) with the man who is, in fact, the candidate who will get most votes; but we do not know which of the candidates he is, *i.e.* we do not know any proposition of the form "A is the candidate who will get most votes" where A is one of the candidates by name. We shall say that we have "merely descriptive knowledge" of the so-and-so when, although we know that the so-and-so exists, and although we may possibly be acquainted with the object which is, in fact, the so-and-so, yet we do not know any proposition "*a* is the so-and-so," where *a* is something with which we are acquainted.

When we say "the so-and-so exists," we

mean that there is just one object which is the so-and-so. The proposition "*a* is the so-and-so" means that *a* has the property so-and-so, and nothing else has. "Mr. A. is the Unionist candidate for this constituency" means "Mr. A. is a Unionist candidate for this constituency, and no one else is." "The Unionist candidate for this constituency exists" means "some one is a Unionist candidate for this constituency, and no one else is." Thus, when we are acquainted with an object which is the so-and-so, we know that the so-and-so exists; but we may know that the so-and-so exists when we are not acquainted with any object which we know to be the so-and-so, and even when we are not acquainted with any object which, in fact, is the so-and-so.

Common words, even proper names, are usually really descriptions. That is to say, the thought in the mind of a person using a proper name correctly can generally only be expressed explicitly if we replace the proper name by a description. Moreover, the description required to express the thought will vary for different people, or for the same person at different times. The only thing constant (so long as the name is rightly used) is the object to which the name applies. But so long as this remains constant, the particular description involved usually makes no difference to the truth or falsehood of the proposition in which the name appears.

Let us take some illustrations. Suppose some statement made about Bismarck. Assuming that there is such a thing as direct acquaintance with oneself, Bismarck himself might have used his name directly to designate the particular person with whom he was acquainted. In this case, if he made a judgment about himself, he himself might be a constituent of the judgment. Here the proper name has the direct use which it always wishes to have, as simply standing for a certain object, and not for a description of the object. But if a person who knew Bismarck made a judgment about him, the case is different. What this person was acquainted with were certain sense-data which he connected (rightly, we will suppose) with Bismarck's body. His body, as a physical object, and still more his mind, were only known as the body and the mind connected with these sense-data. That is, they were known by description. It is, of course, very much a matter of chance which characteristics of a man's appearance will come into a friend's mind when he thinks of him; thus the description actually in the friend's mind is accidental. The essential point is that he knows that the various descriptions all apply to the same entity, in spite of not being acquainted with the entity in question.

When we, who did not know Bismarck, make a judgment about him, the description in our minds will probably be some more or less vague mass of historical knowledge—far more, in most cases, than is required to identify him. But, for the sake of illustration, let us assume that we think of him as "the first Chancellor of the German Empire." Here all the words are abstract except "German." The word "German" will, again, have different meanings for different people. To some it will recall travels in Germany, to some the look of Germany on the map, and so on. But if we are to obtain a description which we know to be applicable, we shall be compelled, at some point, to bring in a reference to a particular with which we are acquainted. Such reference is involved in any mention of past, present, and future (as opposed to definite dates), or of here and there, or of what others have told us. Thus it would seem that, in some way or other, a description known to be applicable to a particular must involve some reference to a particular with which we are acquainted, if our knowledge about the thing described is not to be merely what follows *logically* from the description. For example, "the most long-lived of men" is a description involving only universals, which must apply to some man, but we can make no judgments concerning this man which involve knowledge about him beyond what the description gives. If, however, we say, "The first Chancellor of the German Empire was an astute diplomatist," we can only be assured of the truth of our judgment in virtue of something with which we are acquainted—usually a testimony heard or read. Apart from the information we convey to others, apart from the fact about the actual Bismarck, which gives importance to our judgment, the thought we really have contains the one or more particulars involved, and otherwise consists wholly of concepts.

All names of places—London, England, Europe, the Earth, the Solar System—similarly involve, when used, descriptions which start from some one or more particulars with which we are acquainted. I suspect that even the Universe, as considered by metaphysics, involves such a connection with particulars. In logic, on the contrary, where we are concerned not merely with what does exist, but with whatever might or could exist or be, no reference to actual particulars is involved.

It would seem that, when we make a statement about something only known by description, we often *intend* to make our statement, not in the form involving the description, but about the actual thing described. That is to say, when we say anything about Bismarck, we should like, if we could, to make the judgment which Bismarck alone can make, namely, the judgment of which he himself is a constituent. In this we are necessarily defeated, since the actual Bismarck is unknown to us. But we know that there is an object B, called Bismarck, and that B was an astute diplomatist. We can thus *describe* the proposition we should like to affirm, namely, "B was an astute diplomatist," where B is the object which was Bismarck. If we are describing Bismarck as "the first Chancellor of the German Empire," the proposition we should like to affirm may be described as "the proposition asserting, concerning the actual object which was the first Chancellor of the German Empire, that this object was an astute diplomatist." What enables us to communicate in spite of the varying descriptions we employ is that we know there is a true proposition concerning the actual Bismarck, and that however we may vary the description (so long as the description is correct) the proposition described is still the same. This proposition, which is described and is known to be true, is what interests us ; but we are not acquainted with the proposition itself, and do not know *it*, though we know it is true.

It will be seen that there are various stages in the removal from acquaintance with particulars: there is Bismarck to people who knew him, Bismarck to those who only know of him through history, the man with the iron mask, the longest-lived of men. These are progressively further removed from acquaintance with particulars; the first comes as near to acquaintance as is possible in regard to another person; in the second, we shall still be said to know "who Bismarck was"; in the third, we do not know who was the man with the iron mask, though we can know many propositions about him which are not logically deducible from the fact that he wore an iron mask; in the fourth, finally, we know nothing beyond what is logically deducible from the definition of the man. There is a similar hierarchy in the region of universals. Many universals, like many particulars, are only known to us by description. But here, as in the case of particulars, knowledge concerning what is known by description is ultimately reducible to knowledge concerning what is known by acquaintance.

The fundamental principle in the analysis of propositions containing descriptions is this: *Every proposition which we can understand must be composed wholly of constituents with which we are acquainted.*

We shall not at this stage attempt to answer all the objections which may be urged against this fundamental principle. For the present, we shall merely point out that, in some way or other, it must be possible to meet these objections, for it is scarcely conceivable that we can make a judgment or entertain a supposition without knowing what it is that we are judging or supposing about. We must attach *some* meaning to the words we use, if we are to speak significantly and not utter mere noise; and the meaning we attach to our words must be something with which we are acquainted. Thus when, for example, we make a statement about Julius Cæsar, it is plain that Julius Cæsar himself is not before our minds, since we are not acquainted with him. We have in mind some *description* of Julius Cæsar: "the man who was assassinated on the Ides of March," "the founder of the Roman Empire," or, perhaps, merely "the man whose name was *Julius Cæsar*." (In this last description, *Julius Cæsar* is a noise or shape with which we are acquainted.) Thus our statement does not mean quite what it seems to mean, but means something involving, instead of Julius Cæsar, some description of him which is composed wholly of particulars and universals with which we are acquainted.

The chief importance of knowledge by description is that it enables us to pass beyond the limits of our private experience. In spite of the fact that we can only know truths which are wholly composed of terms which we have experienced in acquaintance, we can yet have knowledge by description of things which we have never experienced. In view of the very narrow range of our immediate experience, this result is vital, and until it is understood, much of our knowledge must remain mysterious and therefore doubtful.

CHAPTER VI

ON INDUCTION

In almost all our previous discussions we have been concerned in the attempt to get clear as to our data in the way of knowledge of existence. What things are there in the universe whose existence is known to us owing to our being acquainted with them? So far, our answer has been that we are acquainted with our sense-data, and, probably, with ourselves. These we know to exist. And past sense-data which are remembered are known to have existed in the past. This knowledge supplies our data.

But if we are to be able to draw inferences from these data—if we are to know of the existence of matter, of other people, of the past before our individual memory begins, or of the future, we must know general principles of some kind by means of which such inferences can be drawn. It must be known to us that the existence of some one sort of thing, A, is a sign of the existence of some other sort of thing, B, either at the same time as A or at some earlier or later time, as, for example, thunder is a sign of the earlier existence of lightning. If this were not known to us, we could never extend our knowledge beyond the sphere of our private experience; and this sphere, as we have seen, is exceedingly limited. The question we have now to consider is whether such an extension is possible, and if so, how it is effected.

Let us take as an illustration a matter about which none of us, in fact, feel the slightest doubt. We are all convinced that the sun will rise to-morrow. Why? Is this belief a mere blind outcome of past experience, or can it be justified as a reasonable belief? It is not easy to find a test by which to judge whether a belief of this kind is reasonable or not, but we can at least ascertain what sort of general beliefs would suffice, if true, to justify the judgment that the sun will rise to-morrow, and the many other similar judgments upon which our actions are based.

It is obvious that if we are asked why we believe that the sun will rise to-morrow, we shall naturally answer, "Because it always has risen every day." We have a firm belief that it will rise in the future, because it has risen in the past. If we are challenged as to why we believe that it will continue to rise as heretofore, we may appeal to the laws of motion: the earth, we shall say, is a freely rotating body, and such bodies do not cease to rotate unless something interferes from outside, and there is nothing outside to interfere with the earth between now and to-morrow. Of course it might be doubted whether we are quite certain that there is nothing outside to interfere, but this is not the interesting doubt. The interesting doubt is as to whether the laws of motion will remain in operation until to-morrow. If this doubt is raised, we find ourselves in the same position as when the doubt about the sunrise was first raised.

The *only* reason for believing that the laws

of motion will remain in operation is that they have operated hitherto, so far as our knowledge of the past enables us to judge. It is true that we have a greater body of evidence from the past in favour of the laws of motion than we have in favour of the sunrise, because the sunrise is merely a particular case of fulfilment of the laws of motion, and there are countless other particular cases. But the real question is: Do *any* number of cases of a law being fulfilled in the past afford evidence that it will be fulfilled in the future? If not, it becomes plain that we have no ground whatever for expecting the sun to rise to-morrow, or for expecting the bread we shall eat at our next meal not to poison us, or for any of the other scarcely conscious expectations that control our daily lives. It is to be observed that all such expectations are only *probable*; thus we have not to seek for a proof that they *must* be fulfilled, but only for some reason in favour of the view that they are *likely* to be fulfilled.

Now in dealing with this question we must, to begin with, make an important distinction, without which we should soon become involved in hopeless confusions. Experience has shown us that, hitherto, the frequent repetition of some uniform succession or coexistence has been a *cause* of our expecting the same succession or coexistence on the next occasion. Food that has a certain appearance generally has a certain taste, and it is a severe shock to our expectations when the familiar appearance is found to be associated with an unusual taste. Things which we see become associated, by habit, with certain tactile sensations which we expect if we touch them; one of the horrors of a ghost (in many ghost-stories) is that it fails to give us any sensations of touch. Uneducated people who go abroad for the first time are so surprised as to be incredulous when they find their native language not understood.

And this kind of association is not confined to men; in animals also it is very strong. A horse which has been often driven along a certain road resists the attempt to drive him in a different direction. Domestic animals expect food when they see the person who usually feeds them. We know that all these rather crude expectations of uniformity are liable to be misleading. The man who has fed the chicken every day throughout its life at last wrings its neck instead, showing that more refined views as to the uniformity of nature would have been useful to the chicken.

But in spite of the misleadingness of such expectations, they nevertheless exist. The mere fact that something has happened a certain number of times causes animals and men to expect that it will happen again. Thus our instincts certainly cause us to believe that the sun will rise to-morrow, but we may be in no better a position than the chicken which unexpectedly has its neck wrung. We have therefore to distinguish the fact that past uniformities *cause* expectations as to the future, from the question whether there is any reasonable ground for giving weight to such expectations after the question of their validity has been raised.

The problem we have to discuss is whether there is any reason for believing in what is called "the uniformity of nature." The belief in the uniformity of nature is the belief that everything that has happened or will happen is an instance of some general law to which there are *no* exceptions. The crude expectations which we have been considering are all subject to exceptions, and therefore liable to disappoint those who entertain them. But science habitually assumes, at least as a working hypothesis, that general rules which have exceptions can be replaced by general rules which have no exceptions. "Unsupported bodies in air fall" is a general rule to which balloons and aeroplanes are exceptions. But the laws of motion and the law of gravitation, which account for the fact that most bodies fall, also account for the fact that balloons and aeroplanes can rise; thus the laws of motion and the law of gravitation are not subject to these exceptions.

The belief that the sun will rise to-morrow might be falsified if the earth came suddenly into contact with a large body which destroyed its rotation; but the laws of motion and the law of gravitation would not be infringed by such an event. The business of science is to find uniformities, such as the laws of motion and the law of gravitation, to which, so far as our experience extends, there are no exceptions. In this search science has been remarkably successful, and it may be conceded that such uniformities have held hitherto. This brings us back to the question: Have we any reason, assuming that they have always held in the past, to suppose that they will hold in the future?

It has been argued that we have reason to know that the future will resemble the past, because what was the future has constantly become the past, and has always been found to resemble the past, so that we really have experience of the future, namely of times which were formerly future, which we may call past futures. But such an argument really begs the very question at issue. We have experience of past futures, but not of future futures, and the question is: Will future futures resemble past futures? This question is not to be answered by an argument which starts from past futures alone. We have therefore still to seek for some principle which shall enable us to know that the future will follow the same laws as the past.

The reference to the future in this question is not essential. The same question arises when we apply the laws that work in our experience to past things of which we have no experience—as, for example, in geology, or in theories as to the origin of the Solar System. The question we really have to ask is: "When two things have been found to be often associated, and no instance is known of the one occurring without the other, does the occurrence of one of the two, in a fresh instance, give any good ground for expecting the other?" On our answer to this question must depend the validity of the whole of our expectations as to the future, the whole of the results obtained by induction, and in fact practically all the beliefs upon which our daily life is based.

It must be conceded, to begin with, that the fact that two things have been found often together and never apart does not, by itself, suffice to *prove* demonstratively that they will be found together in the next case we examine. The most we can hope is that the oftener things are found together, the more probable it becomes that they will be found together another time, and that, if they have been found together often enough, the probability will amount *almost* to certainty. It can never quite reach certainty, because we know that in spite of frequent repetitions there sometimes is a failure at the last, as in the case of the chicken whose neck is wrung. Thus probability is all we ought to seek.

It might be urged, as against the view we are advocating, that we know all natural phenomena to be subject to the reign of law, and that sometimes, on the basis of observation, we can see that only one law can possibly fit the facts of the case. Now to this view there are two answers. The first is that, even if *some* law which has no exceptions applies to our case, we can never, in practice, be sure that we have discovered that law and not one to which there are exceptions. The second is that the reign of law would seem to be itself only probable, and that our belief that it will hold in the future, or in unexamined cases in the past, is itself based upon the very principle we are examining.

The principle we are examining may be called the *principle of induction*, and its two parts may be stated as follows:

(*a*) When a thing of a certain sort A has been found to be associated with a thing of a certain other sort B, and has never been found dissociated from a thing of the sort B, the greater the number of cases in which A and B have been associated, the greater is the probability that they will be associated in a fresh case in which one of them is known to be present;

(*b*) Under the same circumstances, a sufficient number of cases of association will make the probability of a fresh association nearly a certainty, and will make it approach certainty without limit.

As just stated, the principle applies only to the verification of our expectation in a single fresh instance. But we want also to know that there is a probability in favour of the general law that things of the sort A are *always* associated with things of the sort B, provided a sufficient number of cases of association are known, and no cases of failure of association are known. The probability of the general law is obviously less than the probability of the particular case, since if the general law is true, the particular case must also be true, whereas the particular case may be true without the general law being true. Nevertheless the probability of the general law is increased by repetitions, just as the probability of the particular case is. We may therefore repeat the two parts of our principle as regards the general law, thus :

(*a*) The greater the number of cases in which a thing of the sort A has been found associated with a thing of the sort B, the more probable it is (if no cases of failure of association are known) that A is always associated with B ;

(*b*) Under the same circumstances, a sufficient number of cases of the association of A with B will make it nearly certain that A is always associated with B, and will make this general law approach certainty without limit.

It should be noted that probability is always relative to certain data. In our case, the data are merely the known cases of co-existence of A and B. There may be other data, which *might* be taken into account, which would gravely alter the probability. For example, a man who had seen a great many white swans might argue, by our principle, that on the data it was *probable* that all swans were white, and this might be a perfectly sound argument. The argument is not disproved by the fact that some swans are black, because a thing may very well happen in spite of the fact that some data render it improbable. In the case of the swans, a man might know that colour is a very variable characteristic in many species of animals, and that, therefore, an induction as to colour is peculiarly liable to error. But this knowledge would be a fresh datum, by no means proving that the probability relatively to our previous data had been wrongly estimated. The fact, therefore, that things often fail to fulfil our expectations is no evidence that our expectations will not *probably* be fulfilled in a given case or a given class of cases. Thus our inductive principle is at any rate not capable of being *disproved* by an appeal to experience.

The inductive principle, however, is equally incapable of being *proved* by an appeal to experience. Experience might conceivably confirm the inductive principle as regards the cases that have been already examined; but as regards unexamined cases, it is the inductive principle alone that can justify any inference from what has been examined to what has not been examined. All arguments which, on the basis of experience, argue as to the future or the unexperienced parts of the past or present, assume the inductive principle; hence we can never use experience to prove the inductive principle without begging the question. Thus we must either accept the inductive principle on the ground of its intrinsic evidence, or forgo all justification of our expectations about the future. If the principle is unsound, we have no reason to expect the sun to rise to-morrow, to expect bread to be more nourishing than a stone, or to expect that if we throw ourselves off the roof we shall fall. When we see what looks like our best friend approaching us, we shall have no reason to suppose that his body is not inhabited by the mind of our worst enemy or of some total stranger. All our conduct is based upon associations which have worked in the past, and which we therefore regard as likely to work in the future; and this likelihood is dependent for its validity upon the inductive principle.

The general principles of science, such as the belief in the reign of law, and the belief that every event must have a cause, are as completely dependent upon the inductive principle as are the beliefs of daily life. All such general principles are believed because mankind have found innumerable instances of their truth, and no instances of their falsehood. But this affords no evidence for their truth in the future, unless the inductive principle is assumed.

Thus all knowledge which, on a basis of

experience, tells us something about what is not experienced, is based upon a belief which experience can neither confirm nor confute, yet which, at least in its more concrete applications, appears to be as firmly rooted in us as many of the facts of experience. The existence and justification of such beliefs—for the inductive principle, as we shall see, is not the only example—raises some of the most difficult and most debated problems of philosophy. We will, in the next chapter, consider briefly what may be said to account for such knowledge, and what is its scope and its degree of certainty.

CHAPTER VII

ON OUR KNOWLEDGE OF GENERAL PRINCIPLES

We saw in the preceding chapter that the principle of induction, while necessary to the validity of all arguments based on experience, is itself not capable of being proved by experience, and yet is unhesitatingly believed by every one, at least in all its concrete applications. In these characteristics the principle of induction does not stand alone. There are a number of other principles which cannot be proved or disproved by experience, but are used in arguments which start from what is experienced.

Some of these principles have even greater evidence than the principle of induction, and the knowledge of them has the same degree of certainty as the knowledge of the existence of sense-data. They constitute the means of drawing inferences from what is given in sensation; and if what we infer is to be true, it is just as necessary that our principles of inference should be true as it is that our data should be true. The principles of inference are apt to be overlooked because of their very obviousness—the assumption involved is assented to without our realising that it is an assumption. But it is very important to realise the use of principles of inference, if a correct theory of knowledge is to be obtained; for our knowledge of them raises interesting and difficult questions.

In all our knowledge of general principles, what actually happens is that first of all we realise some particular application of the principle, and then we realise that the particularity is irrelevant, and that there is a generality which may equally truly be affirmed. This is of course familiar in such matters as teaching arithmetic: "two and two are four" is first learnt in the case of some particular pair of couples, and then in some other particular case, and so on, until at last it becomes possible to see that it is true of *any* pair of couples.

The same thing happens with logical principles. Suppose two men are discussing what day of the month it is. One of them says, "At least you will admit that *if* yesterday was the 15th to-day must be the 16th." "Yes," says the other, "I admit that." "And you know," the first continues, "that yesterday was the 15th, because you dined with Jones, and your diary will tell you that was on the 15th." "Yes," says the second; "therefore to-day *is* the 16th."

Now such an argument is not hard to follow; and if it is granted that its premisses are true in fact, no one will deny that the conclusion must also be true. But it depends for its truth upon an instance of a general logical principle. The logical principle is as follows: "Suppose it known that *if* this is true, then that is true. Suppose it also known that this *is* true, then it follows that that is true." When it is the case that if this is true, that is true, we shall say that this "implies" that, and that that "follows from" this. Thus our principle states that if this implies that, and this is true, then that is true. In other words, "anything implied by a true proposition is truc," or "whatever follows from a true proposition is truc."

This principle is really involved—at least, concrete instances of it are involved—in all demonstrations. Whenever one thing which we believe is used to prove something else, which we consequently believe, this principle is relevant. If any one asks: "Why should I accept the results of valid arguments based on true premisses?" we can only answer by appealing to our principle. In fact, the truth of the principle is impossible to doubt, and its obviousness is so great that at first sight it seems almost trivial. Such principles, however, are not trivial to the philosopher, for they show that we may have indubitable knowledge which is in no way derived from objects of sense.

The above principle is merely one of a certain number of self-evident logical principles. Some at least of these principles must be granted before any argument or proof becomes possible. When some of them have been granted, others can be proved, though these others, so long as they are simple, are just as obvious as the principles taken for granted. For no very good reason, three of these principles have been singled out by tradition under the name of "Laws of Thought."

They are as follows:

(1) *The law of identity:* "Whatever is, is."

(2) *The law of contradiction:* "Nothing can both be and not be."

(3) *The law of excluded middle:* "Everything must either be or not be."

These three laws are samples of self-evident logical principles, but are not really more fundamental or more self-evident than various other similar principles: for instance, the one we considered just now, which states that what follows from a true premiss is true. The name "laws of thought" is also misleading, for what is important is not the fact that we think in accordance with these laws, but the fact that things behave in accordance with them; in other words, the fact that when we think in accordance with them we think *truly.* But this is a large question, to which we must return at a later stage.

In addition to the logical principles which enable us to prove from a given premiss that something is *certainly* true, there are other logical principles which enable us to prove, from a given premiss, that there is a greater or less probability that something is true. An example of such principles—perhaps the most important example—is the inductive principle, which we considered in the preceding chapter.

One of the great historic controversies in philosophy is the controversy between the two schools called respectively "empiricists" and "rationalists." The empiricists—who are best represented by the British philosophers, Locke, Berkeley, and Hume—maintained that all our knowledge is derived from experience; the rationalists—who are represented by the Continental philosophers of the seventeenth century, especially Descartes and Leibniz—maintained that, in addition to what we know by experience, there are certain "innate ideas" and "innate principles," which we know independently of experience. It has now become possible to decide with some confidence as to the truth or falsehood of these opposing schools. It must be admitted, for the reasons already stated, that logical principles are known to us, and cannot be themselves proved by experience, since all proof presupposes them. In this, therefore, which was the most important point of the controversy, the rationalists were in the right.

On the other hand, even that part of our knowledge which is *logically* independent of experience (in the sense that experience cannot prove it) is yet elicited and caused by experience. It is on occasion of particular experiences that we become aware of the general laws which their connections exemplify. It would certainly be absurd to suppose that there are innate principles in the sense that babies are born with a knowledge of everything which men know and which cannot be deduced from what is experienced. For this reason, the word "innate" would not now be employed to describe our knowledge of logical principles. The phrase "*a priori*" is less objectionable, and is more usual in modern writers. Thus, while admitting that all knowledge is elicited and caused by experience, we shall nevertheless hold that some knowledge is *a priori*, in the sense that the experience which makes us think of it does not suffice to prove it, but merely so directs our attention that we see its truth without requiring any proof from experience.

There is another point of great importance, in which the empiricists were in the right as against the rationalists. Nothing can be known to *exist* except by the help of experience. That is to say, if we wish to prove that something of which we have no direct experience exists, we must have among our premisses the existence of one or more things of which we have direct experience. Our belief that the Emperor of Russia exists, for example, rests upon testimony, and testimony consists, in the last analysis, of sense-data seen or heard in reading or being spoken to. Rationalists believed that, from general consideration as to what *must* be, they could deduce the existence of this or that in the actual world. In this belief they seem to have been mistaken. All the knowledge that we can acquire *a priori* concerning existence seems to be hypothetical: it tells us that *if* one thing exists, another must exist, or, more generally, that *if* one proposition is true, another must be true. This is exemplified by the principles we have already dealt with, such as "*if* this is true, and this implies that, then that is true," or "*if* this and that have been repeatedly found connected, they will probably be connected in the next instance in which one of them is found." Thus the scope and power of *a priori* principles is strictly limited. All knowledge that something exists must be in part dependent on experience. When anything is known immediately, its existence is known by experience alone; when anything is proved to exist, without being known immediately, both experience and *a priori* principles must be required in the proof. Knowledge is called *empirical* when it rests wholly or partly upon experience. Thus all knowledge which asserts existence is empirical, and the only *a priori* knowledge concerning existence is hypothetical, giving connections among things that exist or may exist, but not giving actual existence.

A priori knowledge is not all of the logical kind we have been hitherto considering. Perhaps the most important example of non-logical *a priori* knowledge is knowledge as to ethical value. I am not speaking of judgments as to what is useful or as to what is virtuous, for such judgments do require empirical premisses; I am speaking of judgments as to the intrinsic desirability of things. If something is useful, it must be useful because it secures some end; the end must, if we have gone far enough, be valuable on its own account, and not merely because it is useful for some further end. Thus all judgments as to what is useful depend upon judgments as to what has value on its own account.

We judge, for example, that happiness is more desirable than misery, knowledge than ignorance, goodwill than hatred, and so on. Such judgments must, in part at least, be immediate and *a priori*. Like our previous *a priori* judgments, they may be *elicited* by experience, and indeed they must be; for it seems not possible to judge whether anything is intrinsically valuable unless we have experienced something of the same kind. But it is fairly obvious that they cannot be *proved* by experience; for the fact that a thing exists or does not exist cannot prove either that it is good that it should exist or that it is bad. The pursuit of this subject belongs to ethics, where the impossibility of deducing what ought to be from what is has to be established. In the present connection, it is only important to realise that knowledge as to what is intrinsically of value is *a priori* in the same sense in which logic is *a priori*, namely in the sense that the truth of such knowledge can be neither proved nor disproved by experience.

All pure mathematics is *a priori*, like logic. This was strenuously denied by the empirical philosophers, who maintained that experience was as much the source of our knowledge of arithmetic as of our knowledge of geography. They maintained that by the repeated experience of seeing two things and two other things, and finding that altogether they made four things, we were led by induction to the conclusion that two things and two other things would *always* make four things altogether. If, however, this were the source of our knowledge that two and two are four, we should proceed differently, in persuading ourselves of its truth, from the way in which we do actually proceed. In fact, a certain number of instances are needed to make us think of two abstractly, rather than of two coins or two books or two people, or two of any other specified kind. But as soon as we are able to divest our thoughts of irrelevant particularity, we become able to *see* the general principle that two and two are four; any one instance is seen to be *typical*, and the examination of other instances becomes unnecessary.*

The same thing is exemplified in geometry. If we want to prove some property of *all* triangles, we draw some one triangle and

* *Cf.* A. N. Whitehead, *Introduction to Mathematics* (Home University Library).

reason about it; but we can avoid making use of any property which it does not share with all other triangles, and thus, from our particular case, we obtain a general result. We do not, in fact, feel our certainty that two and two are four increased by fresh instances, because, as soon as we have seen the truth of this proposition, our certainty becomes so great as to be incapable of growing greater. Moreover, we feel some quality of *necessity* about the proposition "two and two are four," which is absent from even the best attested empirical generalisations. Such generalisations always remain mere facts: we feel that there might be a world in which they were false, though in the actual world they happen to be true. In any possible world, on the contrary, we feel that two and two would be four: this is not a mere fact, but a necessity to which everything actual and possible must conform.

The case may be made clearer by considering a genuinely empirical generalisation, such as "All men are mortal." It is plain that we believe this proposition, in the first place, because there is no known instance of men living beyond a certain age, and in the second place because there seem to be physiological grounds for thinking that an organism such as a man's body must sooner or later wear out. Neglecting the second ground, and considering merely our experience of men's mortality, it is plain that we should not be content with one quite clearly understood instance of a man dying, whereas, in the case of "two and two are four," one instance does suffice, when carefully considered, to persuade us that the same must happen in any other instance. Also we can be forced to admit, on reflection, that there may be some doubt, however slight, as to whether *all* men are mortal. This may be made plain by the attempt to imagine two different worlds, in one of which there are men who are not mortal, while in the other two and two make five. When Swift invites us to consider the race of Struldbugs who never die, we are able to acquiesce in imagination. But a world where two and two make five seems quite on a different level. We feel that such a world, if there were one, would upset the whole fabric of our knowledge and reduce us to utter doubt.

The fact is that, in simple mathematical judgments such as "two and two are four," and also in many judgments of logic, we can know the general proposition without inferring it from instances, although some instance is usually necessary to make clear to us what the general proposition means. This is why there is real utility in the process of *deduction*, which goes from the general to the general or from the general to the particular, as well as in the process of *induction*, which goes from the particular to the particular, or from the particular to the general. It is an old debate among philosophers whether deduction ever gives *new* knowledge. We can now see that in certain cases, at least, it does do so. If we already know that two and two always make four, and we know that Brown and Jones are two, and so are Robinson and Smith, we can deduce that Brown and Jones and Robinson and Smith are four. This is new knowledge, not contained in our premisses, because the general proposition, "two and two are four," never told us there were such people as Brown and Jones and Robinson and Smith, and the particular premisses did not tell us that there were four of them, whereas the particular proposition deduced does tell us both these things.

But the newness of the knowledge is much less certain if we take the stock instance of deduction that is always given in books on logic, namely, "All men are mortal; Socrates is a man, therefore Socrates is mortal." In this case, what we really know beyond reasonable doubt is that certain men, A, B, C, were mortal, since, in fact, they have died. If Socrates is one of these men, it is foolish to go the roundabout way through "all men are mortal" to arrive at the conclusion that *probably* Socrates is mortal. If Socrates is not one of the men on whom our induction is based, we shall still do better to argue straight from our A, B, C, to Socrates, than to go round by the general proposition. "all men are mortal." For the probability that Socrates is mortal is greater, on our data, than the probability that all men are mortal.

(This is obvious, because if all men are mortal, so is Socrates; but if Socrates is mortal, it does not follow that all men are mortal.) Hence we shall reach the conclusion that Socrates is mortal with a greater approach to certainty if we make our argument purely inductive than if we go by way of "all men are mortal" and then use deduction.

This illustrates the difference between general propositions known *a priori*, such as "two and two are four," and empirical generalisations such as "all men are mortal." In regard to the former, deduction is the right mode of argument, whereas in regard to the latter, induction is always theoretically preferable, and warrants a greater confidence in the truth of our conclusion, because all empirical generalisations are more uncertain than the instances of them.

We have now seen that there are propositions known *a priori*, and that among them are the propositions of logic and pure mathematics, as well as the fundamental propositions of ethics. The question which must next occupy us is this: How is it possible that there should be such knowledge ? And more particularly, how can there be knowledge of general propositions in cases where we have not examined all the instances, and indeed never can examine them all, because their number is infinite ? These questions, which were first brought prominently forward by the German philosopher Kant (1724–1804), are very difficult, and historically very important.

CHAPTER VIII

HOW *A PRIORI* KNOWLEDGE IS POSSIBLE

IMMANUEL KANT is generally regarded as the greatest of the modern philosophers. Though he lived through the Seven Years' War and the French Revolution, he never interrupted his teaching of philosophy at Königsberg in East Prussia. His most distinctive contribution was the invention of what he called the "critical" philosophy, which, assuming as a datum that there is knowledge of various kinds, inquired how such knowledge comes to be possible, and deduced, from the answer to this inquiry, many metaphysical results as to the nature of the world. Whether these results were valid may well be doubted. But Kant undoubtedly deserves credit for two things: first, for having perceived that we have *a priori* knowledge which is not purely "analytic," *i.e.* such that the opposite would be self-contradictory; and secondly, for having made evident the philosophical importance of the theory of knowledge.

Before the time of Kant, it was generally held that whatever knowledge was *a priori* must be "analytic." What this word means will be best illustrated by examples. If I say, "A bald man is a man," "A plane figure is a figure," "A bad poet is a poet," I make a purely analytic judgment: the subject spoken about is given as having at least two properties, of which one is singled out to be asserted of it. Such propositions as the above are trivial, and would never be enunciated in real life except by an orator preparing the way for a piece of sophistry. They are called "analytic" because the predicate is obtained by merely analysing the subject. Before the time of Kant it was thought that all judgments of which we could be certain *a priori* were of this kind: that in all of them there was a predicate which was only part of the subject of which it was asserted. If this were so, we should be involved in a definite contradiction if we attempted to deny anything that could be known *a priori.* "A bald man is not bald" would assert and deny baldness of the same man, and would therefore contradict itself. Thus according to the philosophers before Kant, the law of contradiction, which asserts that nothing can at the same time have and not have a certain property, sufficed to establish the truth of all *a priori* knowledge.

Hume (1711–1776), who preceded Kant, accepting the usual view as to what makes knowledge *a priori*, discovered that, in many cases which had previously been supposed analytic, and notably in the case of cause and effect, the connection was really synthetic. Before Hume, rationalists at least had supposed that the effect could be logically deduced from the cause, if only we had sufficient knowledge. Hume argued—correctly, as would now be generally admitted—that this could not be done. Hence he inferred the far more doubtful proposition that nothing could be known *a priori* about the connection of cause and effect. Kant, who had been educated in the rationalist tradition, was much perturbed by Hume's scepticism, and endeavoured to find an answer to it. He perceived that not only the connection of cause and effect, but all the propositions of arithmetic and geometry, are "synthetic," *i.e.* not analytic: in all these propositions, no analysis of the subject will reveal the predicate. His stock instance was the proposition $7 + 5 = 12$. He pointed out, quite truly, that 7 and 5 have to be put together to give 12: the idea of 12 is not *contained* in them, nor even in the idea of adding them together. Thus he was led to the conclusion that all pure mathematics, though *a priori*, is synthetic; and this conclusion raised a new problem of which he endeavoured to find the solution.

The question which Kant put at the beginning of his philosophy, namely "How is pure mathematics possible?" is an interesting and difficult one, to which every philosophy which is not purely sceptical must find some answer. The answer of the pure empiricists, that our mathematical knowledge is derived by induction from particular instances, we have already seen to be inadequate, for two reasons: first, that the validity of the inductive principle itself cannot be proved by induction; secondly, that the general propositions of mathematics, such as "two and two always make four," can obviously be known with certainty by consideration of a single instance, and gain nothing by enumeration of other cases in which they have been found to be true. Thus our knowledge of the general propositions of mathematics (and the same applies to logic) must be accounted for otherwise than our (merely probable) knowledge of empirical generalisations such as "all men are mortal."

The problem arises through the fact that such knowledge is general, whereas all experience is particular. It seems strange that we should apparently be able to know some truths in advance about particular things of which we have as yet no experience; but it cannot easily be doubted that logic and arithmetic will apply to such things. We do not know who will be the inhabitants of London a hundred years hence; but we know that any two of them and any other two of them will make four of them. This apparent power of anticipating facts about things of which we have no experience is certainly surprising. Kant's solution of the problem, though not valid in my opinion, is interesting. It is, however, very difficult, and is differently understood by different philosophers. We can, therefore, only give the merest outline of it, and even that will be thought misleading by many exponents of Kant's system.

What Kant maintained was that in all our experience there are two elements to be distinguished, the one due to the object (*i.e.* to what we have called the "physical object"), the other due to our own nature. We saw, in discussing matter and sense-data, that the physical object is different from the associated sense-data, and that the sense-data are to be regarded as resulting from an interaction between the physical object and ourselves. So far, we are in agreement with Kant. But what is distinctive of Kant is the way in which he apportions the shares of ourselves and the physical object respectively. He considers that the crude material given in sensation — the colour, hardness, etc.—is due to the object, and that what we supply is the arrangement in space and time, and all the relations between sense-data which result from comparison or from considering one as the cause of the other or in any other way. His chief reason in favour of this view is that we seem to have *a priori* knowledge as to space and time and causality and comparison, but not as to the actual crude material of sensation. We can be sure, he says, that anything we shall ever experience must show the characteristics affirmed of it in our *a priori* knowledge, because these characteristics are due to our own nature, and therefore nothing can ever come into our experience without acquiring these characteristics.

The physical object, which he calls the "thing in itself," * he regards as essentially unknowable; what can be known is the object as we have it in experience, which he calls the "phenomenon." The phenomenon, being a joint product of us and the thing in itself, is sure to have those characteristics which are due to us, and is therefore sure to conform to our *a priori* knowledge. Hence this knowledge, though true of all actual and possible experience, must not be supposed to apply outside experience. Thus in spite of the existence of *a priori* knowledge, we cannot know anything about the thing in itself or about what is not an actual or possible object of experience. In this way he tries to reconcile and harmonise the contentions of the rationalists with the arguments of the empiricists.

Apart from minor grounds on which Kant's philosophy may be criticised, there is

* Kant's "thing in itself" is identical *in definition* with the physical object, namely, it is the cause of sensation. In the properties deduced from the definition it is not identical, since Kant held (in spite of some inconsistency as regards cause) that we can know that none of the categories are applicable to the "thing in itself."

one main objection which seems fatal to any attempt to deal with the problem of *a priori* knowledge by his method. The thing to be accounted for is our certainty that the facts must always conform to logic and arithmetic. To say that logic and arithmetic are contributed by us does not account for this. Our nature is as much a fact of the existing world as anything, and there can be no certainty that it will remain constant. It might happen, if Kant is right, that to-morrow our nature would so change as to make two and two become five. This possibility seems never to have occurred to him, yet it is one which utterly destroys the certainty and universality which he is anxious to vindicate for arithmetical propositions. It is true that this possibility, formally, is inconsistent with the Kantian view that time itself is a form imposed by the subject upon phenomena, so that our real Self is not in time and has no to-morrow. But he will still have to suppose that the time-order of phenomena is determined by characteristics of what is behind phenomena, and this suffices for the substance of our argument.

Reflection, moreover, seems to make it clear that, if there is any truth in our arithmetical beliefs, they must apply to things equally whether we think of them or not. Two physical objects and two other physical objects must make four physical objects, even if physical objects cannot be experienced. To assert this is certainly within the scope of what we mean when we state that two and two are four. Its truth is just as indubitable as the truth of the assertion that two phenomena and two other phenomena make four phenomena. Thus Kant's solution unduly limits the scope of *a priori* propositions, in addition to failing in the attempt at explaining their certainty.

Apart from the special doctrines advocated by Kant, it is very common among philosophers to regard what is *a priori* as in some sense mental, as concerned rather with the way we must think than with any fact of the outer world. We noted in the preceding chapter the three principles commonly called "laws of thought." The view which led to their being so named is a natural one, but there are strong reasons for thinking that it is erroneous. Let us take as an illustration the law of contradiction. This is commonly stated in the form "Nothing can both be and not be," which is intended to express the fact that nothing can at once have and not have a given quality. Thus, for example, if a tree is a beech it cannot also be not a beech; if my table is rectangular it cannot also be not rectangular, and so on.

Now what makes it natural to call this principle a law of *thought* is that it is by thought rather than by outward observation that we persuade ourselves of its necessary truth. When we have seen that a tree is a beech, we do not need to look again in order to ascertain whether it is also not a beech; thought alone makes us know that this is impossible. But the conclusion that the law of contradiction is a law of *thought* is nevertheless erroneous. What we believe, when we believe the law of contradiction, is not that the mind is so made that it must believe the law of contradiction. *This* belief is a subsequent result of psychological reflection, which presupposes the belief in the law of contradiction. The belief in the law of contradiction is a belief about things, not only about thoughts. It is not, *e.g.*, the belief that if we *think* a certain tree is a beech, we cannot at the same time *think* that it is not a beech; it is the belief that if the tree *is* a beech, it cannot at the same time *be* not a beech. Thus the law of contradiction is about things, and not merely about thoughts; and although belief in the law of contradiction is a thought, the law of contradiction itself is not a thought, but a fact concerning the things in the world. If this, which we believe when we believe the law of contradiction, were not true of the things in the world, the fact that we were compelled to *think* it true would not save the law of contradiction from being false; and this shows that the law is not a law of *thought*.

A similar argument applies to any other *a priori* judgment. When we judge that two and two are four, we are not making a judgment about our thoughts, but about all actual or possible couples. The fact that our minds are so constituted as to believe that two and two are four, though it is true, is emphatically not what we assert when we assert that two and two are four. And no fact about the constitution of our minds could make it *true* that two and two are four. Thus our *a priori* knowledge, if it is not erroneous, is not merely knowledge about the constitution of our minds, but is applicable to whatever the world may contain, both what is mental and what is non-mental.

The fact seems to be that all our *a priori* knowledge is concerned with entities which do not, properly speaking, *exist*, either in the mental or in the physical world. These entities are such as can be named by parts of speech which are not substantives; they are such entities as qualities and relations. Suppose, for instance, that I am in my room. I exist, and my room exists; but does "in" exist? Yet obviously the word "in" has a meaning; it denotes a relation which holds between me and my room. This relation is something, although we cannot say that it exists *in the same sense* in which I and my room exist. The relation "in" is something which we can think about and understand, for, if we could not understand it, we could not understand the sentence "I am in my room." Many philosophers, following Kant, have maintained that relations are the work of the mind, that things in themselves have no relations, but that the mind brings them together in one act of thought and thus produces the relations which it judges them to have.

This view, however, seems open to objections similar to those which we urged before against Kant. It seems plain that it is not thought which produces the truth of the proposition "I am in my room." It may be true that an earwig is in my room, even if neither I nor the earwig nor any one else is aware of this truth; for this truth concerns only the earwig and the room, and does not depend upon anything else. Thus relations, as we shall see more fully in the next chapter, must be placed in a world which is neither mental nor physical. This world is of great importance to philosophy, and in particular to the problems of *a priori* knowledge. In the next chapter we shall proceed to develop its nature and its bearing upon the questions with which we have been dealing.

CHAPTER IX

THE WORLD OF UNIVERSALS

AT the end of the preceding chapter we saw that such entities as relations appear to have a being which is in some way different from that of physical objects, and also different from that of minds and from that of sense-data. In the present chapter we have to consider what is the nature of this kind of being, and also what objects there are that have this kind of being. We will begin with the latter question.

The problem with which we are now concerned is a very old one, since it was brought into philosophy by Plato. Plato's "theory of ideas" is an attempt to solve this very problem, and in my opinion it is one of the most successful attempts hitherto made. The theory to be advocated in what follows is largely Plato's, with merely such modifications as time has shown to be necessary.

The way the problem arose for Plato was more or less as follows. Let us consider, say, such a notion as *justice.* If we ask ourselves what justice is, it is natural to proceed by considering this, that, and the other just act, with a view to discovering what they have in common. They must all, in some sense, partake of a common nature, which will be found in whatever is just and in nothing else. This common nature, in virtue of which they are all just, will be justice itself, the pure essence the admixture of which with facts of ordinary life produces the multiplicity of just acts. Similarly with any other word which may be applicable to common facts, such as "whiteness" for example. The word will be applicable to a number of particular things because they all participate in a common nature or essence. This pure essence is what Plato calls an "idea" or "form." (It must not be supposed that "ideas," in his sense, exist in minds, though they may be apprehended by minds.) The "idea" *justice* is not identical with anything that is just: it is something other than particular things, which particular things partake of. Not being particular, it cannot itself exist in the world of sense. Moreover it is not fleeting or changeable like the things of sense: it is eternally itself, immutable and indestructible.

Thus Plato is led to a supra-sensible world, more real than the common world of sense, the unchangeable world of ideas, which alone gives to the world of sense whatever pale reflection of reality may belong to it. The truly real world, for Plato, is the world of ideas; for whatever we may attempt to say about things in the world of sense, we can only succeed in saying that they participate in such and such ideas, which, therefore, constitute all their character. Hence it is easy to pass on into a mysticism. We may hope, in a mystic illumination, to *see* the ideas as we see objects of sense; and we may imagine that the ideas exist in heaven. These mystical developments are very natural, but the basis of the theory is in logic, and it is as based in logic that we have to consider it.

The word "idea" has acquired, in the course of time, many associations which are quite misleading when applied to Plato's "ideas." We shall therefore use the word "universal" instead of the word "idea," to describe what Plato meant. The essence of the sort of entity that Plato meant is that it is opposed to the particular things that are given in sensation. We speak of whatever is given in sensation, or is of the same nature as things given in sensation, as a *particular*; by opposition to this, a *universal* will be anything which may be shared by many particulars, and has those characteristics which, as we saw, distinguish justice and whiteness from just acts and white things.

When we examine common words, we find that, broadly speaking, proper names stand for particulars, while other substantives, adjectives, prepositions, and verbs stand for universals. Pronouns stand for particulars, but are ambiguous: it is only by the context or the circumstances that we know what particulars they stand for. The word "now" stands for a particular, namely the present moment; but like pronouns, it stands for an ambiguous particular, because the present is always changing.

It will be seen that no sentence can be made up without at least one word which denotes a universal. The nearest approach would be some such statement as "I like this." But even here the word "like" denotes a universal, for I may like other things, and other people may like things. Thus all truths involve universals, and all knowledge of truths involves acquaintance with universals.

Seeing that nearly all the words to be found in the dictionary stand for universals, it is strange that hardly anybody except students of philosophy ever realises that there are such entities as universals. We do not naturally dwell upon those words in a sentence which do not stand for particulars; and if we are forced to dwell upon a word which stands for a universal, we naturally think of it as standing for some one of the particulars that come under the universal. When, for example, we hear the sentence, "Charles I.'s head was cut off," we may naturally enough think of Charles I., of Charles I.'s head, and of the operation of cutting off *his* head, which are all particulars; but we do not naturally dwell upon what is meant by the word "head" or the word "cut," which is a universal. We feel such words to be incomplete and insubstantial; they seem to demand a context before anything can be done with them. Hence we succeed in avoiding all notice of universals as such, until the study of philosophy forces them upon our attention.

Even among philosophers, we may say, broadly, that only those universals which are named by adjectives or substantives have been much or often recognised, while those named by verbs and prepositions have been usually overlooked. This omission has had a very great effect upon philosophy; it is hardly too much to say that most metaphysics, since Spinoza, has been largely determined by it. The way this has occurred is, in outline, as follows: Speaking generally, adjectives and common nouns express qualities or properties of single things, whereas prepositions and verbs tend to express relations between two or more things. Thus the neglect of prepositions and verbs led to the belief that every proposition can be regarded as attributing a property to a single thing, rather than as expressing a relation between two or more things. Hence it was supposed that, ultimately, there can be no such entities as relations between things. Hence either there can be only one thing in the universe, or, if there are many things, they cannot possibly interact in any way, since any interaction would be a relation, and relations are impossible.

The first of these views, which was advocated by Spinoza, and is held in our own day by Mr. Bradley and many other philosophers, is called *monism*; the second, which was advocated by Leibniz, but is not very common nowadays, is called *monadism*, because each of the isolated things is called a *monad*. Both these opposing philosophies, interesting as they are, result, in my opinion, from an undue attention to one sort of universals, namely the sort represented by adjectives and substantives rather than by verbs and prepositions.

As a matter of fact, if any one were anxious to deny altogether that there are such things as universals, we should find that we cannot strictly prove that there are such entities as *qualities*, *i.e.* the universals represented by adjectives and substantives, whereas we can prove that there must be *relations*, *i.e.* the sort of universals generally represented by verbs and prepositions. Let us take in illustration the universal *whiteness*. If we believe that there is such a universal, we shall say that things are white because they have the quality of whiteness. This view, however, was strenuously denied by Berkeley and Hume, who have been followed in this by later empiricists. The form which their denial took was to deny that there are such things as "abstract ideas." When we want to think of whiteness, they said, we form an image of some particular white thing, and reason concerning this particular, taking care not to deduce anything concerning it which we cannot see to be equally true of any other white thing. As an account of our actual mental processes, this is no doubt largely true. In geometry, for example, when we wish to prove something about all triangles, we draw a particular triangle and reason about it, taking care not to use any characteristic which it does not share with other triangles. The beginner, in order to avoid error, often finds it useful to draw several triangles, as unlike each other as possible, in order to make sure that his reasoning is equally applicable to all of them. But a difficulty emerges as soon as we ask ourselves how we know that a thing is white or a triangle. If we wish to avoid the universals *whiteness* and *triangularity*, we shall choose some particular patch of white or some particular triangle, and say that anything is white or a triangle if it has the right sort of resemblance to our chosen particular. But then the resemblance required will have to be a universal. Since there are many white things, the resemblance must hold between many pairs of particular white things; and this is the characteristic of a universal. It will be useless to say that there is a different resemblance for each pair, for then we shall have to say that these resemblances resemble each other, and thus at last we shall be forced to admit resemblance as a universal. The relation of resemblance, therefore, must be a true universal. And having been forced to admit this universal, we find that it is no longer worth while to invent difficult and unplausible theories to avoid the admission of such universals as whiteness and triangularity.

Berkeley and Hume failed to perceive this refutation of their rejection of "abstract ideas," because, like their adversaries, they only thought of *qualities*, and altogether ignored *relations* as universals. We have therefore here another respect in which the rationalists appear to have been in the right as against the empiricists, although, owing to the neglect or denial of relations, the deductions made by rationalists were, if anything, more apt to be mistaken than those made by empiricists.

Having now seen that there must be such entities as universals, the next point to be proved is that their being is not merely mental. By this is meant that whatever being belongs to them is independent of their being thought of or or in any way apprehended by minds. We have already touched on this subject at the end of the preceding chapter, but we must now consider more fully what sort of being it is that belongs to universals.

Consider such a proposition as "Edinburgh is north of London." Here we have a relation between two places, and it seems plain that the relation subsists independently of our knowledge of it. When we come to know that Edinburgh is north of London, we come to know something which has to do only with Edinburgh and London: we do not cause the truth of the proposition by coming to know it, on the contrary we merely apprehend a fact which was there before we knew it. The part of the earth's surface where Edinburgh stands would be north of the part where London stands, even if there were no human being to know about north and south, and even if there were no minds at all in the universe. This is, of course, denied by many philosophers, either for Berkeley's reasons or for Kant's. But we have already considered these reasons, and decided that they are inadequate. We may therefore now assume it to be true that nothing mental is presupposed in the fact that Edinburgh is north of London. But this fact involves the relation "north of," which is a universal; and it would be impossible for the whole fact to involve nothing mental if the relation "north of," which is a constituent part of the fact, did involve anything mental. Hence we must admit that the relation, like the terms it relates, is not dependent upon thought, but belongs to the independent world which thought apprehends but does not create.

This conclusion, however, is met by the difficulty that the relation "north of" does not seem to *exist* in the same sense in which Edinburgh and London exist. If we ask "Where and when does this relation exist?" the answer must be "Nowhere and nowhen." There is no place or time where we can find the relation "north of." It does not exist in Edinburgh any more than in London, for it relates the two and is neutral as between them. Nor can we say that it exists at any particular time. Now everything that can be apprehended by the senses or by introspection exists at some particular time. Hence the relation "north of" is radically different from such things. It is neither in space nor in time, neither material nor mental; yet it is something.

It is largely the very peculiar kind of being that belongs to universals which has led many people to suppose that they are really mental. We can think *of* a universal, and our thinking then exists in a perfectly ordinary sense, like any other mental act. Suppose, for example, that we are thinking of whiteness. Then *in one sense* it may be said that whiteness is "in our mind." We have here the same ambiguity as we noted in discussing Berkeley in Chapter IV. In the strict sense, it is not whiteness that is in our mind, but the act of thinking of whiteness. The connected ambiguity in the word "idea," which we noted at the same time, also causes confusion here. In one sense of this word, namely the sense in which it denotes the *object* of an act of thought, whiteness is an "idea." Hence, if the ambiguity is not guarded against, we may come to think that whiteness is an "idea" in the other sense, *i.e.* an act of thought; and thus we come to think that whiteness is mental. But in so thinking, we rob it of its essential quality of universality. One man's act of thought is necessarily a different thing from another man's; one man's act of thought at one time is necessarily a different thing from the same man's act of thought at another time. Hence, if whiteness were the thought as opposed to its object, no two different men could think of it, and no one man could think of it twice. That which many different thoughts of whiteness have in common is their *object*, and this object is different from all of them. Thus universals are not thoughts, though when known they are the objects of thoughts.

We shall find it convenient only to speak of things *existing* when they are in time, that is to say, when we can point to some time *at* which they exist (not excluding the possibility of their existing at all times). Thus thoughts and feelings, minds and physical objects *exist*. But universals do not exist in this sense; we shall say that they *subsist* or *have being*, where "being" is opposed to "existence" as being timeless. The world of universals, therefore, may also be described as the world of being. The world of being is unchangeable, rigid, exact, delightful to the mathematician, the logician, the builder of metaphysical systems, and all who love perfection more than life. The world of existence is fleeting, vague, without sharp boundaries, without any clear plan or arrangement, but it contains all thoughts and feelings, all the data of sense, and all physical objects, everything that can do either good or harm, everything that makes any difference to the value of life and the world. According to our temperaments, we shall prefer the contemplation of the one or of the other. The one we do not prefer will probably seem to us a pale shadow of the one we prefer, and hardly worthy to be regarded as in any sense real. But the truth is that both have the same claim on our impartial attention, both are real, and both are important to the metaphysician. Indeed no sooner have we distinguished the two worlds than it becomes necessary to consider their relations.

But first of all we must examine our knowledge of universals. This consideration will occupy us in the following chapter, where we shall find that it solves the problem of *a priori* knowledge, from which we were first led to consider universals.

CHAPTER X

ON OUR KNOWLEDGE OF UNIVERSALS

In regard to one man's knowledge at a given time, universals, like particulars, may be divided into those known by acquaintance, those known only by description, and those not known either by acquaintance or by description.

Let us consider first the knowledge of universals by acquaintance. It is obvious, to begin with, that we are acquainted with such universals as white, red, black, sweet, sour, loud, hard, etc., *i.e.* with qualities which are exemplified in sense-data. When we see a white patch, we are acquainted, in the first instance, with the particular patch; but by seeing many white patches, we easily learn to abstract the whiteness which they all have in common, and in learning to do this we are learning to be acquainted with whiteness. A similar process will make us acquainted with any other universal of the same sort. Universals of this sort may be called "sensible qualities." They can be apprehended with less effort of abstraction than any others, and they seem less removed from particulars than other universals are.

We come next to relations. The easiest relations to apprehend are those which hold between the different parts of a single complex sense-datum. For example, I can see at a glance the whole of the page on which I am writing; thus the whole page is included in one sense-datum. But I perceive that some parts of the page are to the left of other parts, and some parts are above other parts. The process of abstraction in this case seems to proceed somewhat as follows: I see successively a number of sense-data in which one part is to the left of another; I perceive, as in the case of different white patches, that all these sense-data have something in common, and by abstraction I find that what they have in common is a certain relation between their parts, namely the relation which I call "being to the left of." In this way I become acquainted with the universal relation.

In like manner I become aware of the relation of before and after in time. Suppose I hear a chime of bells: when the last bell of the chime sounds, I can retain the whole chime before my mind, and I can perceive that the earlier bells came before the later ones. Also in memory I perceive that what I am remembering came before the present time. From either of these sources I can abstract the universal relation of before and after, just as I abstracted the universal relation "being to the left of." Thus time-relations, like space-relations, are among those with which we are acquainted.

Another relation with which we become acquainted in much the same way is resemblance. If I see simultaneously two shades of green, I can see that they resemble each other; if I also see a shade of red at the same time, I can see that the two greens have more resemblance to each other than either has to the red. In this way I become acquainted with the universal *resemblance* or *similarity*.

Between universals, as between particulars, there are relations of which we may be immediately aware. We have just seen that we can perceive that the resemblance between two shades of green is greater than the resemblance between a shade of red and a shade of green. Here we are dealing with a relation, namely "greater than," between two relations. Our knowledge of such relations, though it requires more power of abstraction than is required for perceiving the qualities of sense-data, appears to be equally immediate, and (at least in some cases) equally indubitable. Thus there is immediate knowledge concerning universals as well as concerning sense-data.

Returning now to the problem of *a priori* knowledge, which we left unsolved when we began the consideration of universals, we find ourselves in a position to deal with it in a much more satisfactory manner than was possible before. Let us revert to the proposition "two and two are four." It is fairly obvious, in view of what has been said, that this proposition states a relation between the universal "two" and the universal "four." This suggests a proposition which we shall now endeavour to establish; namely, *All* a priori *knowledge deals exclusively with the relations of universals.* This proposition is of great importance, and goes a long way towards solving our previous difficulties concerning *a priori* knowledge.

The only case in which it might seem, at first sight, as if our proposition were untrue, is the case in which an *a priori* proposition states that *all* of one class of particulars belong to some other class, or (what comes to the same thing) that *all* particulars having some one property also have some other. In this case it might seem as though we were dealing with the particulars that have the property rather than with the property. The proposition "two and two are four" is really a case in point, for this may be stated in the form "any two and any other two are four," or "any collection formed of two twos is a collection of four." If we can show that such statements as this really deal only with universals, our proposition may be regarded as proved.

One way of discovering what a proposition deals with is to ask ourselves what words we must understand—in other words, what objects we must be acquainted with—in order to see what the proposition means. As soon as we see what the proposition means, even if we do not yet know whether it is true or false, it is evident that we must have acquaintance with whatever is really dealt with by the proposition. By applying this test, it appears that many propositions which might seem to be concerned with particulars are really concerned only with universals. In the special case of "two and two are four," even when we interpret it as meaning "any collection formed of two twos is a collection of four," it is plain that we can *understand* the proposition, *i.e.* we can see what it is that it asserts, as soon as we know what is meant by "collection" and "two" and "four." It is quite unnecessary to know all the couples in the world: if it were necessary, obviously we could never understand the proposition, since the couples are infinitely numerous and therefore cannot all be known to us. Thus although our general statement *implies* statements about particular couples, *as soon as we know that there are such particular couples*, yet it does not itself assert or imply that there are such particular couples, and thus fails to make any statement whatever about any actual particular couple. The statement made is about "couple," the universal, and not about this or that couple.

Thus the statement "two and two are four" deals exclusively with universals, and therefore may be known by anybody who is acquainted with the universals concerned and can perceive the relation between them which the statement asserts. It must be taken as a fact, discovered by reflecting upon our knowledge, that we have the power of sometimes perceiving such relations between universals, and therefore of sometimes knowing general *a priori* propositions such as those of arithmetic and logic. The thing that seemed mysterious, when we formerly considered such knowledge, was that it seemed to anticipate and control experience. This, however, we can now see to have been an error. *No* fact concerning anything capable of being experienced can be known independently of experience. We know *a priori* that two things and two other things together make four things, but we do *not* know *a priori* that if Brown and Jones are two, and Robinson and Smith are two, then Brown and Jones and Robinson and Smith are four. The reason is that this proposition cannot be understood at all unless we know that there are such people as Brown and Jones and Robinson and Smith, and this we can only know by experience. Hence, although our general proposition is *a priori*, all its applications to actual particulars involve experience and therefore contain an empirical element. In this way what seemed mysterious in our *a priori* knowledge is seen to have been based upon an error.

It will serve to make the point clearer if we contrast our genuine *a priori* judgment with an empirical generalisation, such as "all men are mortals." Here as before, we can *understand* what the proposition mcans as soon as we understand the universals involved, namely *man* and *mortal*. It is obviously unnecessary to have an individual acquaintance with the whole human race in order to understand what our proposition means. Thus the difference between an *a priori* general proposition and an empirical generalisation does not come in the *meaning* of the proposition; it comes in the nature of the *evidence* for it. In thc empirical case, the evidence consists in the particular instances. We believe that all men are mortal because we know that there are innumerable instances of men dying, and no instances of thcir living beyond a certain age. We do not believe it because we see a connection between the universal *man* and the universal *mortal*. It is true that if physiology can prove, assuming the general laws that govern living bodies, that no living organism can last for ever, that gives a connection between *man* and *mortality* which would enable us to assert our proposition without appealing to the special evidence of *men* dying. But that only means that our generalisation has been subsumed under a wider generalisation, for which the evidence is still of the same kind, though more extensive. The progress of science is constantly producing such subsumptions, and therefore giving a constantly wider inductive basis for scientific generalisations. But although this gives a greater *degree* of certainty, it does not give a different *kind*: the ultimate ground remains inductive, *i.e.* derived from instances, and not an *a priori* connection of universals such as we have in logic and arithmetic.

Two opposite points are to be observed concerning *a priori* general propositions. The first is that, if many particular instances are known, our general proposition may be arrived at in the first instance by induction, and the connection of universals may be only subsequently perceived. For example, it is known that if we draw perpendiculars to the sides of a triangle from the opposite angles, all three perpendiculars meet in a point. It would be quite possible to be first led to this proposition by actually drawing perpendiculars in many cases, and finding that they always met in a point; this experience might lead us to look for the general proof and find it. Such cases are common in the experience of every mathematician.

The other point is more interesting, and of more philosophical importance. It is, that we may sometimes know a general proposition in cases where we do not know a single instance of it. Take such a case as the following: We know that any two numbers can be multiplied together, and will give a third called their *product*. We know that all pairs of integers the product of which is less than 100 have been actually multiplied together, and the value of the product recorded in the multiplication table. But we also know that the number of integers is infinite, and that only a finite number of pairs of integers ever have been or ever will be thought of by human beings. Hence it follows that there are pairs of integers which never have been and never will be thought of by human beings, and that all of them deal with integers the product of which is over 100. Hence we arrive at the proposition: "All products of two integers, which never have been and never will be thought of by any human being, are over 100." Here is a general proposition of which the truth is undeniable, and yet, from the very nature of the case, we can never give an instance; because any two numbers we may think of are excluded by the terms of the proposition.

This possibility, of knowledge of general propositions of which no instance can be given, is often denied, because it is not perceived that the knowledge of such propositions only requires a knowledge of the relations of universals, and does not require any knowledge of instances of the universals in question. Yet the knowledge of such general propositions is quite vital to a great deal of what is generally admitted to be known. For example, we saw, in our early chapters, that physical objects, as opposed to sense-data, are only obtained by an inference, and are not things with which we are acquainted. Hence we can never know any proposition of the form "this is a physical object," where "this" is something immediately known. It follows that all our knowledge concerning physical objects is such that no actual instance can be given. We can give instances of the associated sense-data, but we cannot give instances of the actual physical objects. Hence our knowledge as to physical objects depends throughout upon this possibility of general knowledge where no instance can be given. And the same applies to our knowledge of other people's minds, or of any other class of things of which no instance is known to us by acquaintance.

We may now take a survey of the sources of our knowledge, as they have appeared in the course of our analysis. We have first to distinguish knowledge of things and knowledge of truths. In each there are two kinds, one immediate and one derivative.

Our immediate knowledge of things, which we called *acquaintance*, consists of two sorts, according as the things known are particulars or universals. Among particulars, we have acquaintance with sense-data and (probably) with ourselves. Among universals, there seems to be no principle by which we can decide which can be known by acquaintance, but it is clear that among those that can be so known are sensible qualities, relations of space and time, similarity, and certain abstract logical universals. Our derivative knowledge of things, which we call knowledge by *description*, always involves both acquaintance with something and knowledge of truths. Our immediate knowledge of *truths* may be called *intuitive* knowledge, and the truths so known may be called *self-evident* truths. Among such truths are included those which merely state what is given in sense, and also certain abstract logical and arithmetical principles, and (though with less certainty) some ethical propositions. Our *derivative* knowledge of truths consists of everything that we can deduce from self-evident truths by the use of self-evident principles of deduction.

If the above account is correct, all our knowledge of truths depends upon our intuitive knowledge. It therefore becomes important to consider the nature and scope of intuitive knowledge, in much the same way as, at an earlier stage, we considered the nature and scope of knowledge by acquaintance. But knowledge of truths raises a further problem, which does not arise in regard to knowledge of things, namely the problem of *error.* Some of our beliefs turn out to be erroneous, and therefore it becomes necessary to consider how, if at all, we can distinguish knowledge from error. This problem does not arise with regard to knowledge by acquaintance, for, whatever may be the object of acquaintance, even in dreams and hallucinations, there is no error involved so long as we do not go beyond the immediate object: error can only arise when we regard the immediate object, *i.e.* the sense-datum, as the mark of some physical object. Thus the problems connected with knowledge of truths are more difficult than those connected with knowledge of things. As the first of the problems connected with knowledge of truths, let us examine the nature and scope of our intuitive judgments.

CHAPTER XI

ON INTUITIVE KNOWLEDGE

THERE is a common impression that everything that we believe ought to be capable of proof, or at least of being shown to be highly probable. It is felt by many that a belief for which no reason can be given is an unreasonable belief. In the main, this view is just. Almost all our common beliefs are either inferred, or capable of being inferred, from other beliefs which may be regarded as giving the reason for them. As a rule, the reason has been forgotten, or has even never been consciously present to our minds. Few of us ever ask ourselves, for example, what reason there is to suppose the food we are just going to eat will not turn out to be poison. Yet we feel, when challenged, that a perfectly good reason could be found, even if we are not ready with it at the moment. And in this belief we are usually justified.

But let us imagine some insistent Socrates, who, whatever reason we give him, continues to demand a reason for the reason. We must sooner or later, and probably before very long, be driven to a point where we cannot find any further reason, and where it becomes almost certain that no further reason is even theoretically discoverable. Starting with the common beliefs of daily life, we can be driven back from point to point, until we come to some general principle, or some instance of a general principle, which seems luminously evident, and is not itself capable of being deduced from anything more evident. In most questions of daily life, such as whether our food is likely to be nourishing and not poisonous, we shall be driven back to the inductive principle, which we discussed in Chapter VI. But beyond that, there seems to be no further regress. The principle itself is constantly used in our reasoning, sometimes consciously, sometimes unconsciously; but there is no reasoning which, starting from some simpler self-evident principle, leads us to the principle of induction as its conclusion. And the same holds for other logical principles. Their truth is evident to us, and we employ them in constructing demonstrations; but they themselves, or at least some of them, are incapable of demonstration.

Self-evidence, however, is not confined to those among general principles which are incapable of proof. When a certain number of logical principles have been admitted, the rest can be deduced from them; but the propositions deduced are often just as self-evident as those that were assumed without proof. All arithmetic, moreover, can be deduced from the general principles of logic, yet the simple propositions of arithmetic, such as "two and two are four," are just as self-evident as the principles of logic.

It would seem, also, though this is more disputable, that there are some self-evident ethical principles, such as "we ought to pursue what is good."

It should be observed that, in all cases of general principles, particular instances, dealing with familiar things, are more evident than the general principle. For example, the law of contradiction states that nothing can both have a certain property and not have it. This is evident as soon as it is understood, but it is not so evident as that a particular rose which we see cannot be both red and not red. (It is of course possible, that parts of the rose may be red and parts not red, or that the rose may be of a shade of pink which we hardly know whether to call red or not; but in the former case it is plain that the rose as a whole is not red, while in the latter case the answer is theoretically definite as soon as we have decided on a precise definition of "red.") It is usually through particular instances that we come to be able to see the general principle. Only those who are practised in dealing with abstractions can readily grasp a general principle without the help of instances.

In addition to general principles, the other kind of self-evident truths are those immediately derived from sensation. We will call such truths "truths of perception," and the judgments expressing them we will call "judgments of perception." But here a certain amount of care is required in getting at the precise nature of the truths that are self-evident. The actual sense-data are neither true nor false. A particular patch of colour which I see, for example, simply exists: it is not the sort of thing that is true or false. It is true that there is such a patch, true that it has a certain shape and degree of brightness, true that it is surrounded by certain other colours. But the patch itself, like everything else in the world of sense, is of a radically different kind from the things that are true or false, and therefore cannot properly be said to be *true*. Thus whatever self-evident truths may be obtained from our senses must be different from the sense-data from which they are obtained.

It would seem that there are two kinds of self-evident truths of perception, though perhaps in the last analysis the two kinds may coalesce. First, there is the kind which simply asserts the *existence* of the sense-datum, without in any way analysing it. We see a patch of red, and we judge "there is such-and-such a patch of red," or more strictly "there is that"; this is one kind of intuitive judgment of perception. The other kind arises when the object of sense is complex, and we subject it to some degree of analysis. If, for instance, we see a *round* patch of red, we may judge "that patch of red is round." This is again a judgment of perception, but it differs from our previous kind. In our present kind we have a single sense-datum which has both colour and shape: the colour is red and the shape is round. Our judgment analyses the datum into colour and shape, and then recombines them by stating that the red colour is round in shape. Another example of this kind of judgment is "this is to the right of that," where "this" and "that" are seen simultaneously. In this kind of judgment the sense-datum contains constituents which have some relation to each other, and the judgment asserts that these constituents have this relation.

Another class of intuitive judgments, analogous to those of sense and yet quite distinct from them, are judgments of *memory*. There is some danger of confusion as to the nature of memory, owing to the fact that memory of an object is apt to be accompanied by an image of the object, and yet the image cannot be what constitutes memory. This is easily seen by merely noticing that the image is in the present, whereas what is remembered is known to be in the past. Moreover, we are certainly able to some extent to compare our image with the object remembered, so that we often know, within somewhat wide limits, how far our image is accurate; but this would be impossible, unless the object, as opposed to the image, were in some way before the mind. Thus the essence of memory is not constituted by the image, but by having immediately before the mind an object which is recognised as past. But for the fact of memory in this sense, we should not know that there ever was a past at all, nor should we be able to understand the word "past," any more than a man born blind can understand the word "light." Thus there must be intuitive judgments of memory, and it is upon them, ultimately, that all our knowledge of the past depends.

The case of memory, however, raises a difficulty, for it is notoriously fallacious, and thus throws doubt on the trustworthiness of intuitive judgments in general. This difficulty is no light one. But let us first narrow its scope as far as possible. Broadly speaking, memory is trustworthy in proportion to the vividness of the experience and to its nearness in time. If the house next door was struck by lightning half a minute ago, my memory of what I saw and heard will be so reliable that it would be preposterous to doubt whether there had been a flash at all. And the same applies to less vivid experiences, so long as they are recent. I am absolutely certain that half a minute ago I was sitting in the same chair in which I am sitting now. Going backward over the day, I find things of which I am quite certain, other things of which I am almost certain, other things of which I can become certain by thought and by calling up attendant circumstances, and some things of which I am by no means certain. I am quite certain that I ate my breakfast this morning, but if I were as indifferent to my breakfast as a philosopher should be, I should be doubtful. As to the conversation at breakfast, I can recall some of it easily, some with an effort, some only with a large element of doubt, and some not at all. Thus there is a continual gradation in the degree of self-evidence of what I remember, and a corresponding gradation in the trustworthiness of my memory.

Thus the first answer to the difficulty of fallacious memory is to say that memory has degrees of self-evidence, and that these correspond to the degrees of its trustworthiness, reaching a limit of perfect self-evidence and perfect trustworthiness in our memory of events which are recent and vivid.

It would seem, however, that there are cases of very firm belief in a memory which is wholly false. It is probable that, in these cases, what is really remembered, in the sense of being immediately before the mind, is something other than what is falsely believed in, though something generally associated with it. George IV. is said to have at last believed that he was at the battle of Waterloo, because he had so often said that he was. In this case, what was immediately remembered was his repeated assertion; the belief in what he was asserting (if it existed) would be produced by association with the remembered assertion, and would therefore not be a genuine case of memory. It would seem that cases of fallacious memory can probably all be dealt with in this way, *i.e.* they can be shown to be not cases of memory in the strict sense at all.

One important point about self-evidence is made clear by the case of memory, and that is, that self-evidence has degrees: it is not a quality which is simply present or absent, but a quality which may be more or less present, in gradations ranging from absolute certainty down to an almost imperceptible faintness. Truths of perception and some of the principles of logic have the very highest degree of self-evidence; truths of immediate memory have an almost equally high degree. The inductive principle has less self-evidence than some of the other principles of logic, such as "what follows from a true premiss must be true." Memories have a diminishing self-evidence as they become remoter and fainter; the truths of logic and mathematics have (broadly speaking) less self-evidence as they become more complicated. Judgments of intrinsic ethical or æsthetic value are apt to have some self-evidence, but not much.

Degrees of self-evidence are important in the theory of knowledge, since, if propositions may (as seems likely) have some degree of self-evidence without being true, it will not be necessary to abandon all connection between self-evidence and truth, but merely to say that, where there is a conflict, the more self-evident proposition is to be retained and the less self-evident rejected.

It seems, however, highly probable that two different notions are combined in "self-evidence" as above explained; that one of them, which corresponds to the highest degree of self-evidence, is really an infallible guarantee of truth, while the other, which corresponds to all the other degrees, does not give an infallible guarantee, but only a greater or less presumption. This, however, is only a suggestion, which we cannot as yet develop further. After we have dealt with the nature of truth, we shall return to the subject of self-evidence, in connection with the distinction between knowledge and error.

CHAPTER XII

TRUTH AND FALSEHOOD

OUR knowledge of truths, unlike our knowledge of things, has an opposite, namely *error*. So far as things are concerned, we may know them or not know them, but there is no positive state of mind which can be described as erroneous knowledge of things, so long, at any rate, as we confine ourselves to knowledge by acquaintance. Whatever we are acquainted with must be something: we may draw wrong inferences from our acquaintance, but the acquaintance itself cannot be deceptive. Thus there is no dualism as regards acquaintance. But as regards knowledge of truths, there is a dualism. We may believe what is false as well as what is true. We know that on very many subjects different people hold different and incompatible opinions: hence some beliefs must be erroneous. Since erroneous beliefs are often held just as strongly as true beliefs, it becomes a difficult question how they are to be distinguished from true beliefs. How are we to know, in a given case, that our belief is not erroneous? This is a question of the very greatest difficulty, to which no completely satisfactory answer is possible. There is, however, a preliminary question which is rather less difficult, and that is: What do we *mean* by truth and falsehood? It is this preliminary question which is to be considered in this chapter.

In this chapter we are not asking how we can know whether a belief is true or false: we are asking what is meant by the question whether a belief is true or false. It is to be hoped that a clear answer to this question may help us to obtain an answer to the question what beliefs are true, but for the present we ask only "What is truth?" and "What is falsehood?" not "What beliefs are true?" and "What beliefs are false?" It is very important to keep these different questions entirely separate, since any confusion between them is sure to produce an answer which is not really applicable to either.

There are three points to observe in the attempt to discover the nature of truth, three requisites which any theory must fulfil.

(1) Our theory of truth must be such as to admit of its opposite, falsehood. A good many philosophers have failed adequately to satisfy this condition: they have constructed theories according to which all our thinking ought to have been true, and have then had the greatest difficulty in finding a place for falsehood. In this respect our theory of belief must differ from our theory of acquaintance, since in the case of acquaintance it was not necessary to take account of any opposite.

(2) It seems fairly evident that if there were no beliefs there could be no falsehood, and no truth either, in the sense in which truth is correlative to falsehood. If we imagine a world of mere matter, there would be no room for falsehood in such a world, and although it would contain what may be

called "facts," it would not contain any truths, in the sense in which truths are things of the same kind as falsehoods. In fact, truth and falsehood are properties of beliefs and statements: hence a world of mere matter, since it would contain no beliefs or statements, would also contain no truth or falsehood.

(3) But, as against what we have just said, it is to be observed that the truth or falsehood of a belief always depends upon something which lies outside the belief itself. If I believe that Charles I. died on the scaffold, I believe truly, not because of any intrinsic quality of my belief, which could be discovered by merely examining the belief, but because of an historical event which happened two and a half centuries ago. If I believe that Charles I. died in his bed, I believe falsely: no degree of vividness in my belief, or of care in arriving at it, prevents it from being false, again because of what happened long ago, and not because of any intrinsic property of my belief. Hence, although truth and falsehood are properties of beliefs, they

are properties dependent upon the relations of the beliefs to other things, not upon any internal quality of the beliefs.

The third of the above requisites leads us to adopt the view—which has on the whole been commonest among philosophers—that truth consists in some form of correspondence between belief and fact. It is, however, by no means an easy matter to discover a form of correspondence to which there are no irrefutable objections. By this partly—and partly by the feeling that, if truth consists in a correspondence of thought with something outside thought, thought can never know when truth has been attained—many philosophers have been led to try to find some definition of truth which shall not consist in relation to something wholly outside belief. The most important attempt at a definition of this sort is the theory that truth consists in *coherence*. It is said that the mark of falsehood is failure to cohere in the body of our beliefs, and that it is the essence of a truth to form part of the completely rounded system which is The Truth.

There is, however, a great difficulty in this view, or rather two great difficulties. The first is that there is no reason to suppose that only *one* coherent body of beliefs is possible. It may be that, with sufficient imagination, a novelist might invent a past for the world that would perfectly fit on to what we know, and yet be quite different from the real past. In more scientific matters, it is certain that there are often two or more hypotheses which account for all the known facts on some subject, and although, in such cases, men of science endeavour to find facts which will rule out all the hypotheses except one, there is no reason why they should always succeed.

In philosophy, again, it seems not uncommon for two rival hypotheses to be both able to account for all the facts. Thus, for example, it is possible that life is one long dream, and that the outer world has only that degree of reality that the objects of dreams have; but although such a view does not seem inconsistent with known facts, there is no reason to prefer it to the common-sense view, according to which other people and things do really exist. Thus coherence as the definition of truth fails because there is no proof that there can be only one coherent system.

The other objection to this definition of truth is that it assumes the meaning of "coherence" known, whereas, in fact, "coherence" presupposes the truth of the laws of logic. Two propositions are coherent when both may be true, and are incoherent when one at least must be false. Now in order to know whether two propositions can both be true, we must know such truths as the law of contradiction. For example, the two propositions "this tree is a beech" and "this tree is not a beech," are not coherent, because of the law of contradiction. But if the law of contradiction itself were subjected to the test of coherence, we should find that, if we choose to suppose it false, nothing will any longer be incoherent with anything else. Thus the laws of logic supply the skeleton or framework within which the test of coherence applies, and they themselves cannot be established by this test.

For the above two reasons, coherence cannot be accepted as giving the *meaning* of truth, though it is often a most important *test* of truth after a certain amount of truth has become known.

Hence we are driven back to *correspondence with fact* as constituting the nature of truth. It remains to define precisely what we mean by "fact," and what is the nature of the correspondence which must subsist between belief and fact, in order that belief may be true.

In accordance with our three requisites, we have to seek a theory of truth which (1) allows truth to have an opposite, namely falsehood, (2) makes truth a property of beliefs, but (3) makes it a property wholly dependent upon the relation of the beliefs to outside things.

The necessity of allowing for falsehood makes it impossible to regard belief as a relation of the mind to a single object, which could be said to be what is believed. If belief were so regarded, we should find that, like acquaintance, it would not admit of the opposition of truth and falsehood, but would have to be always true. This may be made clear by examples. Othello believes falsely that Desdemona loves Cassio. We cannot say that this belief consists in a relation to a single object, " Desdemona's love for Cassio," for if there were such an object, the belief would be true. There is in fact no such object, and therefore Othello cannot have any relation to such an object. Hence his belief cannot possibly consist in a relation to this object.

It might be said that his belief is a relation to a different object, namely " that Desdemona loves Cassio "; but it is almost as difficult to suppose that there is such an object as this, when Desdemona does not love Cassio, as it was to suppose that there is " Desdemona's love for Cassio." Hence it will be better to seek for a theory of belief which does not make it consist in a relation of the mind to a single object.

It is common to think of relations as though they always held between *two* terms, but in fact this is not always the case. Some relations demand three terms, some four, and so on. Take, for instance, the relation "between." So long as only two terms come in, the relation "between" is impossible: three terms are the smallest number that render it possible. York is between London and Edinburgh; but if London and Edinburgh were the only places in the world, there could be nothing which was between one place and another. Similarly *jealousy* requires three people: there can be no such relation that does not involve three at least. Such a proposition as "A wishes B to promote C's marriage with D" involves a relation of four terms; that is to say, A and B and C and D all come in, and the relation involved cannot be expressed otherwise than in a form involving all four. Instances might be multiplied indefinitely, but enough has been said to show that there are relations which require more than two terms before they can occur.

The relation involved in *judging* or *believing* must, if falsehood is to be duly allowed for, be taken to be a relation between several terms, not between two. When Othello believes that Desdemona loves Cassio, he must not have before his mind a single object, "Desdemona's love for Cassio," or "that Desdemona loves Cassio," for that would require that there should be objective falsehoods, which subsist independently of any minds; and this, though not logically refutable, is a theory to be avoided if possible. Thus it is easier to account for falsehood if we take judgment to be a relation in which the mind and the various objects concerned all occur severally; that is to say, Desdemona and loving and Cassio must all be terms in the relation which subsists when Othello believes that Desdemona loves Cassio. This relation, therefore, is a relation of four terms, since Othello also is one of the terms of the relation. When we say that it is a relation of four terms, we do not mean that Othello has a certain relation to Desdemona, and has the same relation to loving and also to Cassio. This may be true of some other relation than believing; but believing, plainly, is not a relation which Othello has to *each* of the three terms concerned, but to *all* of them together: there is only one example of the relation of believing involved, but this one example knits together four terms. Thus the actual occurrence, at the moment when Othello is entertaining his belief, is that the relation called "believing" is knitting together into one complex whole the four terms Othello, Desdemona, loving, and Cassio. What is called belief or judgment is nothing but this relation of believing or judging, which relates a mind to several things other than itself. An *act* of belief or of judgment is the occurrence between certain terms at some particular time, of the relation of believing or judging.

We are now in a position to understand what it is that distinguishes a true judgment from a false one. For this purpose we will adopt certain definitions. In every act of judgment there is a mind which judges, and there are terms concerning which it judges. We will call the mind the *subject* in the judgment, and the remaining terms the *objects*. Thus, when Othello judges that Desdemona loves Cassio, Othello is the subject, while the objects are Desdemona and loving and Cassio. The subject and the objects together are called the *constituents* of the judgment. It will be observed that the relation of judging has what is called a "sense" or "direction." We may say, metaphorically, that it puts its objects in a certain *order*, which we may indicate by means of the order of the words in the sentence. (In an inflected language, the same thing will be indicated by inflections, *e.g.* by the difference between nominative and accusative.) Othello's judgment that Cassio loves Desdemona differs from his judgment that Desdemona loves Cassio, in spite of the fact that it consists of the same constituents, because the relation of judging places the constituents in a different order in the two cases. Similarly, if Cassio judges that Desdemona loves Othello, the constituents of the judgment are still the same, but their order is different. This property of having a "sense" or "direction" is one which the relation of judging shares with all other relations. The "sense" of relations is the ultimate source of order and series and a host of mathematical concepts; but we need not concern ourselves further with this aspect.

We spoke of the relation called "judging" or "believing" as knitting together into one complex whole the subject and the objects. In this respect, judging is exactly like every other relation. Whenever a relation holds between two or more terms, it unites the terms into a complex whole. If Othello loves Desdemona, there is such a complex whole as "Othello's love for Desdemona." The terms united by the relation may be themselves complex, or may be simple, but the whole which results from their being united must be complex. Wherever there is a relation which relates certain terms, there is a complex object formed of the union of those terms; and conversely, wherever there is a complex object, there is a relation which relates its constituents. When an act of believing occurs, there is a complex, in which "believing" is the uniting relation, and subject and objects are arranged in a certain order by the "sense" of the relation of believing. Among the objects, as we saw in considering "Othello believes that Desdemona loves Cassio," one must be a relation—in this instance, the relation "loving." But this relation, as it occurs in the act of believing, is not the relation which creates the unity of the complex whole consisting of the subject and the objects. The relation "loving," as it occurs in the act of believing, is one of the objects—it is a brick in the structure, not the cement. The cement is the relation "believing." When the belief is *true*, there is another complex unity, in which the relation which was one of the objects of the belief relates the other objects. Thus, *e.g.*, if Othello believes *truly* that Desdemona loves Cassio, then there is a complex unity, "Desdemona's love for Cassio," which is composed exclusively of the *objects* of the belief, in the same order as they had in the belief, with the relation which was one of the objects occurring now as the cement that binds together the other objects of the belief. On the other hand, when a belief is *false*, there is no such complex unity composed only of the objects of the belief. If Othello believes *falsely* that Desdemona loves Cassio, then there is no such complex unity as "Desdemona's love for Cassio."

Thus a belief is *true* when it *corresponds* to a certain associated complex, and *false* when it does not. Assuming, for the sake of definiteness, that the objects of the belief are two terms and a relation, the terms being put in a certain order by the "sense" of the believing, then if the two terms in that order are united by the relation into a complex, the belief is true; if not, it is false. This constitutes the definition of truth and falsehood that we were in search of. Judging or believing is a certain complex unity of which a mind is a constituent; if the remaining constituents, taken in the order which they have in the belief, form a complex unity, then the belief is true; if not, it is false.

Thus although truth and falsehood are properties of beliefs, yet they are in a sense extrinsic properties, for the condition of the truth of a belief is something not involving beliefs, or (in general) any mind at all, but only the *objects* of the belief. A mind, which believes, believes truly when there is a *corresponding* complex not involving the mind, but only its objects. This correspondence ensures truth, and its absence entails falsehood. Hence we account simultaneously for the two facts that beliefs (*a*) depend on minds for their *existence*, (*b*) do not depend on minds for their *truth*.

We may restate our theory as follows: If we take such a belief as "Othello believes that Desdemona loves Cassio," we will call Desdemona and Cassio the *object-terms*, and loving the *object-relation*. If there is a complex unity "Desdemona's love for Cassio," consisting of the object-terms related by the object-relation in the same order as they have in the belief, then this complex unity is called the *fact corresponding to the belief*. Thus a belief is true when there is a corresponding fact, and is false when there is no corresponding fact.

It will be seen that minds do not *create* truth or falsehood. They create beliefs, but when once the beliefs are created, the mind cannot make them true or false, except in the special case where they concern future things which are within the power of the person believing, such as catching trains. What makes a belief true is a *fact*, and this fact does not (except in exceptional cases) in any way involve the mind of the person who has the belief.

Having now decided what we *mean* by truth and falsehood, we have next to consider what ways there are of knowing whether this or that belief is true or false. This consideration will occupy the next chapter.

CHAPTER XIII

KNOWLEDGE, ERROR, AND PROBABLE OPINION

The question as to what we mean by truth and falsehood, which we considered in the preceding chapter, is of much less interest than the question as to how we can know what is true and what is false. This question will occupy us in the present chapter. There can be no doubt that *some* of our beliefs are erroneous; thus we are led to inquire what certainty we can ever have that such and such a belief is not erroneous. In other words, can we ever *know* anything at all, or do we merely sometimes by good luck believe what is true? Before we can attack this question, we must, however, first decide what we mean by "knowing," and this question is not so easy as might be supposed.

At first sight we might imagine that knowledge could be defined as "true belief." When what we believe is true, it might be supposed that we had achieved a knowledge of what we believe. But this would not accord with the way in which the word is commonly used. To take a very trivial instance: If a man believes that the late Prime Minister's last name began with a B, he believes what is true, since the late Prime Minister was Sir Henry Campbell Bannerman. But if he believes that Mr. Balfour was the late Prime Minister, he will still believe that the late Prime Minister's last name began with a B, yet this belief, though true, would not be thought to constitute knowledge. If a newspaper, by an intelligent anticipation, announces the result of a battle before any telegram giving the result has been received, it may by good fortune announce what afterwards turns out to be the right result, and it may produce belief in some of its less experienced readers. But in spite of the truth of their belief, they cannot be said to have knowledge. Thus it is clear that a true belief is not knowledge when it is deduced from a false belief.

In like manner, a true belief cannot be called knowledge when it is deduced by a fallacious process of reasoning, even if the premisses from which it is deduced are true. If I know that all Greeks are men and that Socrates was a man, and I infer that Socrates was a Greek, I cannot be said to *know* that Socrates was a Greek, because, although my premisses and my conclusion are true, the conclusion does not follow from the premisses.

But are we to say that nothing is knowledge except what is validly deduced from true premisses? Obviously we cannot say this. Such a definition is at once too wide and too narrow. In the first place, it is too wide, because it is not enough that our premisses should be *true*, they must also be *known*. The man who believes that Mr. Balfour was the late Prime Minister may proceed to draw valid deductions from the true premiss that the late Prime Minister's name began with a B, but he cannot be said to *know* the conclusions reached by these deductions. Thus we shall have to amend our definition by saying that knowledge is what is validly deduced from *known* premisses. This, however, is a circular definition: it assumes that we already know what is meant by "known premisses." It can, therefore, at best define one sort of knowledge, the sort we call derivative, as opposed to intuitive knowledge. We may say: "*Derivative* knowledge is what is validly deduced from premisses known intuitively." In this statement there is no formal defect, but it leaves the definition of *intuitive* knowledge still to seek.

Leaving on one side, for the moment, the question of intuitive knowledge, let us consider the above suggested definition of derivative knowledge. The chief objection to it is that it unduly limits knowledge. It constantly happens that people entertain a true belief, which has grown up in them because of some piece of intuitive knowledge from which it is capable of being validly inferred, but from which it has not, as a matter of fact, been inferred by any logical process.

Take, for example, the beliefs produced by

reading. If the newspapers announce the death of the King, we are fairly well justified in believing that the King is dead, since this is the sort of announcement which would not be made if it were false. And we are quite amply justified in believing that the newspaper asserts that the King is dead. But here the intuitive knowledge upon which our belief is based is knowledge of the existence of sense-data derived from looking at the print which gives the news. This knowledge scarcely rises into consciousness, except in a person who cannot read easily. A child may be aware of the shapes of the letters, and pass gradually and painfully to a realisation of their meaning. But anybody accustomed to reading passes at once to what the letters mean, and is not aware, except on reflection, that he has derived this knowledge from the sense-data called seeing the printed letters. Thus although a valid inference from the letters to their meaning is possible, and *could* be performed by the reader, it is not in fact performed, since he does not in fact perform any operation which can be called logical inference. Yet it would be absurd to say that the reader does not *know* that the newspaper announces the King's death.

We must, therefore, admit as derivative knowledge whatever is the result of intuitive knowledge even if by mere association, provided there *is* a valid logical connection, and the person in question could become aware of this connection by reflection. There are in fact many ways, besides logical inference, by which we pass from one belief to another: the passage from the print to its meaning illustrates these ways. These ways may be called "psychological inference." We shall, then, admit such psychological inference as a means of obtaining derivative knowledge, provided there is a discoverable logical inference which runs parallel to the psychological inference. This renders our definition of derivative knowledge less precise than we could wish, since the word "discoverable" is vague: it does not tell us how much reflection may be needed in order to make the discovery. But in fact "knowledge" is not a precise conception: it merges into "probable opinion," as we shall see more fully in the course of the present chapter. A very precise definition, therefore, should not be sought, since any such definition must be more or less misleading.

The chief difficulty in regard to knowledge, however, does not arise over derivative knowledge, but over intuitive knowledge. So long as we are dealing with derivative knowledge, we have the test of intuitive knowledge to fall back upon. But in regard to intuitive beliefs, it is by no means easy to discover any criterion by which to distinguish some as true and others as erroneous. In this question it is scarcely possible to reach any very precise result: all our knowledge of truths is infected with *some* degree of doubt, and a theory which ignored this fact would be plainly wrong. Something may be done, however, to mitigate the difficulties of the question.

Our theory of truth, to begin with, supplies the possibility of distinguishing certain truths as *self-evident* in a sense which ensures infallibility. When a belief is true, we said, there is a corresponding fact, in which the several objects of the belief form a single complex. The belief is said to constitute *knowledge* of this fact, provided it fulfils those further somewhat vague conditions which we have been considering in the present chapter. But in regard to any fact, besides the knowledge constituted by belief, we may also have the kind of knowledge constituted by *perception* (taking this word in its widest possible sense). For example, if you know the hour of the sunset, you can at that hour know the fact that the sun is setting : this is knowledge of the fact by way of knowledge of *truths* ; but you can also, if the weather is fine, look to the west and actually see the setting sun : you then know the same fact by the way of knowledge of *things*.

Thus in regard to any complex fact, there are, theoretically, two ways in which it may be known : (1) by means of a judgment, in which its several parts are judged to be related as they are in fact related ; (2) by means of *acquaintance* with the complex fact itself, which may (in a large sense) be called perception, though it is by no means confined to objects of the senses. Now it will be observed that the second way of knowing a complex fact, the way of acquaintance, is only possible when there really is such a fact, while the first way, like all judgment, is liable to error. The second way gives us the complex whole, and is therefore only possible when its parts do actually have that relation which makes them combine to form such a complex. The first way, on the contrary, gives us the parts and the relation severally, and demands only the reality of the parts and the relation: the relation may not relate those parts in that way, and yet the judgment may occur.

It will be remembered that at the end of Chapter XI we suggested that there might be two kinds of self-evidence, one giving an absolute guarantee of truth, the other only a partial guarantee. These two kinds can now be distinguished.

We may say that a truth is self-evident, in the first and most absolute sense, when we have acquaintance with the fact which corresponds to the truth. When Othello believes that Desdemona loves Cassio, the corresponding fact, if his belief were true, would be "Desdemona's love for Cassio." This would be a fact with which no one could have acquaintance except Desdemona; hence in the sense of self-evidence that we are considering, the truth that Desdemona loves Cassio (if it were a truth) could only be self-evident to Desdemona. All mental facts, and all facts concerning sense-data, have this same privacy: there is only one person to whom they can be self-evident in our present sense, since there is only one person who can be acquainted with the mental things or the sense-data concerned. Thus no fact about any particular existing thing can be self-evident to more than one person. On the other hand, facts about universals do not have this privacy. Many minds may be acquainted with the same universals; hence a relation between universals may be known by acquaintance to many different people. In all cases where we know by acquaintance a complex fact consisting of certain terms in a certain relation, we say that the truth that these terms are so related has the first or absolute kind of self-evidence, and in these cases the judgment that the terms are so related *must* be true. Thus this sort of self-evidence is an absolute guarantee of truth.

But although this sort of self-evidence is an absolute guarantee of truth, it does not enable us to be *absolutely* certain, in the case of any given judgment, that the judgment in question is true. Suppose we first perceive the sun shining, which is a complex fact, and thence proceed to make the judgment "the sun is shining." In passing from the perception to the judgment, it is necessary to analyse the given complex fact: we have to separate out "the sun" and "shining" as constituents of the fact. In this process it is possible to commit an error; hence even where a *fact* has the first or absolute kind of self-evidence, a judgment believed to correspond to the fact is not absolutely infallible, because it may not really correspond to the fact. But if it does correspond (in the sense explained in the preceding chapter), then it *must* be true.

The second sort of self-evidence will be that

which belongs to judgments in the first instance, and is not derived from direct perception of a fact as a single complex whole. This second kind of self-evidence will have degrees, from the very highest degree down to a bare inclination in favour of the belief. Take, for example, the case of a horse trotting away from us along a hard road. At first our certainty that we hear the hoofs is complete; gradually, if we listen intently, there comes a moment when we think perhaps it was imagination or the blind upstairs or our own heart-beats; at last we become doubtful whether there was any noise at all; then we *think* we no longer hear anything, and at last we *know* we no longer hear anything. In this process, there is a continual gradation of self-evidence, from the highest degree to the least, not in the sense-data themselves, but in the judgments based on them.

Or again: Suppose we are comparing two shades of colour, one blue and one green. We can be quite sure they are different shades of colour; but if the green colour is gradually altered to be more and more like the blue, becoming first a blue-green, then a greeny-blue, then blue, there will come a moment when we are doubtful whether we can see any difference, and then a moment when we know that we cannot see any difference. The same thing happens in tuning a musical instrument, or in any other case where there is a continuous gradation. Thus self-evidence of this sort is a matter of degree; and it seems plain that the higher degrees are more to be trusted than the lower degrees.

In derivative knowledge our ultimate premisses must have some degree of self-evidence, and so must their connection with the conclusions deduced from them. Take for example a piece of reasoning in geometry. It is not enough that the axioms from which we start should be self-evident: it is necessary also that, at each step in the reasoning, the connection of premiss and conclusion should be self-evident. In difficult reasoning, this connection has often only a very small degree of self-evidence; hence errors of reasoning are not improbable where the difficulty is great.

From what has been said it is evident that, both as regards intuitive knowledge and as regards derivative knowledge, if we assume that intuitive knowledge is trustworthy in proportion to the degree of its self-evidence, there will be a gradation in trustworthiness, from the existence of noteworthy sense-data and the simpler truths of logic and arithmetic, which may be taken as quite certain, down to judgments which seem only just more probable than their opposites. What we firmly believe, if it is true, is called *knowledge*, provided it is either intuitive or inferred (logically or psychologically) from intuitive knowledge from which it follows logically. What we firmly believe, if it is not true, is called *error*. What we firmly believe, if it is neither knowledge nor error, and also what we believe hesitatingly, because it is, or is derived from, something which has not the highest degree of self-evidence, may be called *probable opinion*. Thus the greater part of what would commonly pass as knowledge is more or less probable opinion.

In regard to probable opinion, we can

derive great assistance from *coherence,* which we rejected as the *definition* of truth, but may often use as a *criterion.* A body of individually probable opinions, if they are mutually coherent, become more probable than any one of them would be individually. It is in this way that many scientific hypotheses acquire their probability. They fit into a coherent system of probable opinions, and thus become more probable than they would be in isolation. The same thing applies to general philosophical hypotheses. Often in a single case such hypotheses may seem highly doubtful, while yet, when we consider the order and coherence which they introduce into a mass of probable opinion, they become pretty nearly certain. This applies, in particular, to such matters as the distinction between dreams and waking life. If our dreams, night after night, were as coherent one with another as our days, we should hardly know whether to believe the dreams or the waking life. As it is, the test of coherence condemns the dreams and confirms the waking life. But this test, though it increases probability wnere it is successful, never gives absolute certainty, unless there is certainty already at some point in the coherent system. Thus the mere organisation of probable opinion will never, by itself, transform it into indubitable knowledge.

CHAPTER XIV

THE LIMITS OF PHILOSOPHICAL KNOWLEDGE

In all that we have said hitherto concerning philosophy, we have scarcely touched on many matters that occupy a great space in the writings of most philosophers. Most philosophers—or, at any rate, very many—profess to be able to prove, by *a priori* metaphysical reasoning, such things as the fundamental dogmas of religion, the essential rationality of the universe, the illusoriness of matter, the unreality of all evil, and so on. There can be no doubt that the hope of finding reason to believe such theses as these has been the chief inspiration of many life-long students of philosophy. This hope, I believe, is vain. It would seem that knowledge concerning the universe as a whole is not to be obtained by metaphysics, and that the proposed proofs that, in virtue of the laws of logic, such and such things *must* exist and such and such others cannot, are not capable of surviving a critical scrutiny. In this chapter we shall briefly consider the kind of way in which such reasoning is attempted, with a view to discovering whether we can hope that it may be valid.

The great representative, in modern times, of the kind of view which we wish to examine, was Hegel (1770–1831). Hegel's philosophy is very difficult, and commentators differ as to the true interpretation of it. According to the interpretation I shall adopt, which is that of many, if not most of the commentators, and has the merit of giving an interesting and important type of philosophy, his main thesis is that everything short of the Whole is obviously fragmentary, and obviously incapable of existing without the complement supplied by the rest of the world. Just as a comparative anatomist, from a single bone, sees what kind of animal the whole must have been, so the metaphysician, according to Hegel, sees, from any one piece of reality, what the whole of reality must be—

at least in its large outlines. Every apparently separate piece of reality has, as it were, hooks which grapple it to the next piece; the next piece, in turn, has fresh hooks, and so on, until the whole universe is reconstructed. This essential incompleteness appears, according to Hegel, equally in the world of thought and in the world of things. In the world of thought, if we take any idea which is abstract or incomplete, we find, on examination, that, if we forget its incompleteness, we become involved in contradictions; these contradictions turn the idea in question into its opposite, or antithesis; and in order to escape, we have to find a new, less incomplete idea, which is the synthesis of our original idea and its antithesis.

This new idea, though less incomplete than the idea we started with, will be found, nevertheless, to be still not wholly complete, but to pass into its antithesis, with which it must be combined in a new synthesis. In this way Hegel advances until he reaches the "Absolute Idea," which, according to him, has no incompleteness, no opposite, and no need of further development. The Absolute Idea, therefore, is adequate to describe Absolute Reality; but all lower ideas only describe reality as it appears to a partial view, not as it is to one who simultaneously surveys the Whole. Thus Hegel reaches the conclusion that Absolute Reality forms one single harmonious system, not in space or time, not in any degree evil, wholly rational, and wholly spiritual. Any appearance to the contrary, in the world we know, can be proved logically—so he believes—to be entirely due to our fragmentary piecemeal view of the universe. If we saw the universe whole, as we may suppose God sees it, space and time and matter and evil and all striving and struggling would disappear, and we should see instead an eternal perfect unchanging spiritual unity.

In this conception, there is undeniably something sublime, something to which we could wish to yield assent. Nevertheless, when the arguments in support of it are carefully examined, they appear to involve much confusion and many unwarrantable assumptions. The fundamental tenet upon which the system is built up is that what is incomplete must be not self-subsistent, but must need the support of other things before it can exist. It is held that whatever has relations to things outside itself must contain some reference to those outside things in its own *nature*, and could not, therefore, be what it is if those outside things did not exist. A man's nature, for example, is constituted by his memories and the rest of his knowledge, by his loves and hatreds, and so on; thus, but for the objects which he knows or loves or hates, he could not be what he is. He is essentially and obviously a fragment: taken as the sum-total of reality he would be self-contradictory.

This whole point of view, however, turns upon the notion of the "nature" of a thing, which seems to mean "all the truths about the thing." It is of course the case that a truth which connects one thing with another thing could not subsist if the other thing did not subsist. But a truth about a thing is not part of the thing itself, although it must, according to the above usage, be part of the "nature" of the thing. If we mean by a thing's "nature" all the truths about the thing, then plainly we cannot know a thing's "nature" unless we know all the thing's relations to all the other things in the universe. But if the word "nature" is used in this sense, we shall have to hold that the thing may be known when its "nature" is not known, or at any rate is not known completely. There is a confusion, when this use of the word "nature" is employed, between knowledge of things and knowledge of truths. We may have knowledge of a thing by acquaintance even if we know very few propositions about it—theoretically we need not know any propositions about it. Thus, acquaintance with a thing does not involve knowledge of its "nature" in the above sense. And although acquaintance with a thing is involved in our knowing any one proposition about a thing, knowledge of its "nature," in the above sense, is not involved. Hence, (1) acquaintance with a thing does not logically involve a knowledge of its relations, and (2) a knowledge of some of its relations does not involve a knowledge of all of its relations nor a knowledge of its "nature" in the above sense. I may be acquainted, for example, with my toothache, and this knowledge may be as complete as knowledge by acquaintance ever can be, without knowing all that the dentist (who is not acquainted with it) can tell me about its cause, and without therefore knowing its "nature" in the above sense. Thus the fact that a thing has relations does not prove that its relations are logically necessary. That is to say, from the mere fact that it is the thing it is we cannot deduce that it must have the various relations which in fact it has. This only *seems* to follow because we know it already.

It follows that we cannot prove that the universe as a whole forms a single harmonious system such as Hegel believes that it forms. And if we cannot prove this, we also cannot prove the unreality of space and time and matter and evil, for this is deduced by Hegel from the fragmentary and relational character of these things. Thus we are left to the piecemeal investigation of the world, and are unable to know the characters of those parts of the universe that are remote from our experience. This result, disappointing as it is to those whose hopes have been raised by the systems of philosophers, is in harmony with the inductive and scientific temper of our age, and is borne out by the whole examination of human knowledge which has occupied our previous chapters.

Most of the great ambitious attempts of metaphysicians have proceeded by the attempt to prove that such and such apparent features of the actual world were self-contradictory, and therefore could not be real. The whole tendency of modern thought, however, is more and more in the direction of showing that the supposed contradictions were illusory, and that very little can be proved *a priori* from considerations of what *must* be. A good illustration of this is afforded by space and time. Space and time appear to be infinite in extent, and infinitely divisible. If we travel along a straight line in either direction, it is difficult to believe that we shall finally reach a last point, beyond which there is nothing, not even empty space. Similarly, if in imagination we travel backwards or forwards in time, it is difficult to believe that we shall reach a first or last time, with not even empty time beyond it. Thus space and time appear to be infinite in extent.

Again, if we take any two points on a line, it seems evident that there must be other points between them, however small the distance between them may be: every distance can be halved, and the halves can be halved again, and so on *ad infinitum*. In time, similarly, however little time may elapse between two moments, it seems evident that there will be other moments between them. Thus space and time appear to be infinitely divisible. But as against these apparent facts —infinite extent and infinite divisibility— philosophers have advanced arguments tending to show that there could be no infinite collections of things, and that therefore the number of points in space, or of instants in time, must be finite. Thus a contradiction emerged between the apparent nature of space and time and the supposed impossibility of infinite collections.

Kant, who first emphasised this contradiction, deduced the impossibility of space and time, which he declared to be merely subjective; and since his time very many philosophers have believed that space and time are mere appearance, not characteristic of the world as it really is. Now, however, owing to the labours of the mathematicians, notably Georg Cantor, it has appeared that the impossibility of infinite collections was a mistake. They are not in fact self-contradictory, but only contradictory of certain rather obstinate mental prejudices. Hence the reasons for regarding spacc and time as unreal have become inoperative, and one of the great sources of metaphysical constructions is dried up.

The mathematicians, however, have not been content with showing that space as it is commonly supposed to be is possible; they have shown also that many other forms of space are equally possible, so far as logic can show. Some of Euclid's axioms, which appear to common sense to be necessary, and were formerly supposed to be necessary by philosophers, are now known to derive their appearance of necessity from our mere familiarity with actual space, and not from any *a priori* logical foundation. By imagining worlds in which these axioms are false, the mathematicians have used logic to loosen the prejudices of common sense, and to show the possibility of spaces differing—some more, some less—from that in which we live. And some of these spaces differ so little from Euclidean space, where distances such as we can measure are concerned, that it is impossible to discover by observation whether our actual space is strictly Euclidean or of one of these other kinds. Thus the position is completely reversed. Formerly it appeared that experience left only one kind of space to logic, and logic showed this one kind to be impossible. Now, logic presents many kinds of space as possible apart from experience, and experience only partially decides between them. Thus, while our knowledge of what is has become less than it was formerly supposed to be, our knowledge of what may be is enormously increased. Instead of being shut in within narrow walls, of which every nook and cranny could be explored, we find ourselves in an open world of free possibilities, where much remains unknown because there is so much to know.

What has happened in the case of space and time has happened, to some extent, in other directions as well. The attempt to prescribe to the universe by means of *a priori* principles has broken down; logic, instead of being, as formerly, the bar to possibilities, has become the great liberator of the imagination, presenting innumerable alternatives which are closed to unreflective common sense, and leaving to experience the task of deciding, where decision is possible, between the many worlds which logic offers for our choice. Thus knowledge as to what exists becomes limited to what we can learn from experience—not to what we can actually experience, for, as we have seen, there is much knowledge by description concerning things of which we have no direct experience. But in all cases of knowledge by description, we need some connection of universals, enabling us, from such and such a datum, to infer an object of a certain sort as implied by our datum. Thus in regard to physical objects, for example, the principle that sense-data are signs of physical objects is itself a connection of universals; and it is only in virtue of this principle that experience enables us to acquire knowledge concerning physical objects. The same applies to the law of causality, or, to descend to what is less general, to such principles as the law of gravitation.

Principles such as the law of gravitation are proved, or rather are rendered highly probable, by a combination of experience with some wholly *a priori* principle, such as the principle of induction. Thus our intuitive knowledge, which is the source of all our other knowledge of truths, is of two sorts: pure empirical knowledge, which tells us of the existence and some of the properties of particular things with which we are acquainted, and pure *a priori* knowledge, which gives us connections between universals, and enables us to draw inferences from the particular facts given in empirical knowledge. Our derivative knowledge always depends upon some pure *a priori* knowledge and usually also depends upon some pure empirical knowledge.

Philosophical knowledge, if what has been said above is true, does not differ essentially from scientific knowledge; there is no special source of wisdom which is open to philosophy but not to science, and the results obtained by philosophy are not radically different from those obtained from science. The essential characteristic of philosophy, which makes it a study distinct from science, is *criticism*. It examines critically the principles employed in science and in daily life; it searches out any inconsistencies there may be in these principles, and it only accepts them when, as the result of a critical inquiry, no reason for rejecting them has appeared. If, as many philosophers have believed, the principles underlying the sciences were capable, when disengaged from irrelevant detail, of giving us knowledge concerning the universe as a whole, such knowledge would have the same claim on our belief as scientific knowledge has; but our inquiry has not revealed any such knowledge, and therefore, as regards the special doctrines of the bolder metaphysicians, has had a mainly negative result. But as regards what would be commonly accepted as knowledge, our result is in the main positive: we have seldom found reason to reject such knowledge as the result of our criticism, and we have seen no reason to suppose man incapable of the kind of knowledge which he is generally believed to possess.

When, however, we speak of philosophy as a *criticism* of knowledge, it is necessary to impose a certain limitation. If we adopt the attitude of the complete sceptic, placing ourselves wholly outside all knowledge, and asking, from this outside position, to be compelled to return within the circle of knowledge, we are demanding what is impossible, and our scepticism can never be refuted. For all refutation must begin with some piece of knowledge which the disputants share; from blank doubt, no argument can begin. Hence the criticism of knowledge which philosophy employs must not be of this destructive kind, if any result is to be achieved. Against this absolute scepticism, no *logical* argument can be advanced. But it is not difficult to see that scepticism of this kind is unreasonable. Descartes' "methodical doubt," with which modern philosophy began, is not of this kind, but is rather the kind of criticism which we are asserting to be the essence of philosophy. His "methodical doubt" consisted in doubting whatever seemed doubtful; in pausing, with each apparent piece of knowledge, to ask himself whether, on reflection, he could feel certain that he really knew it. This is the kind of criticism which constitutes philosophy. Some knowledge, such as knowledge of the existence of our sense-data, appears quite indubitable, however calmly and thoroughly we reflect upon it. In regard to such knowledge, philosophical criticism does not require that we should abstain from belief. But there are beliefs—such, for example, as the belief that physical objects exactly resemble our sense-data—which are entertained until we begin to reflect, but are found to melt away when subjected to a close inquiry. Such beliefs philosophy will bid us reject, unless some new line of argument is found to support them. But to reject the beliefs which do not appear open to any objections, however closely we examine them, is not reasonable, and is not what philosophy advocates.

The criticism aimed at, in a word, is not that which, without reason, determines to reject, but that which considers each piece of apparent knowledge on its merits, and retains whatever still appears to be knowledge when this consideration is completed. That some risk of error remains must be admitted, since human beings are fallible. Philosophy may claim justly that it diminishes the risk of error, and that in some cases it renders the risk so small as to be practically negligible. To do more than this is not possible in a world where mistakes must occur ; and more than this no prudent advocate of philosophy would claim to have performed.

CHAPTER XV

THE VALUE OF PHILOSOPHY

HAVING now come to the end of our brief and very incomplete review of the problems of philosophy, it will be well to consider, in conclusion, what is the value of philosophy and why it ought to be studied. It is the more necessary to consider this question, in view of the fact that many men, under the influence of science or of practical affairs, are inclined to doubt whether philosophy is anything better than innocent but useless trifling, hair-splitting distinctions, and controversies on matters concerning which knowledge is impossible.

This view of philosophy appears to result, partly from a wrong conception of the ends of life, partly from a wrong conception of the kind of goods which philosophy strives to achieve. Physical science, through the medium of inventions, is useful to innumerable people who are wholly ignorant of it; thus the study of physical science is to be recommended, not only, or primarily, because of the effect on the student, but rather because of the effect on mankind in general. This utility does not belong to philosophy. If the study of philosophy has any value at all for others than students of philosophy, it must be only indirectly, through its effects upon the lives of those who study it. It is in these effects, therefore, if anywhere, that the value of philosophy must be primarily sought.

But further, if we are not to fail in our endeavour to determine the value of philosophy, we must first free our minds from the prejudices of what are wrongly called "practical" men. The "practical" man, as this word is often used, is one who recognises only material needs, who realises that men must have food for the body, but is oblivious of the necessity of providing food for the mind. If all men were well off, if poverty and disease had been reduced to their lowest possible point, there would still remain much to be done to produce a valuable society; and even in the existing world the goods of the mind are at least as important as the goods of the body. It is exclusively among the goods of the mind that the value of philosophy is to be found; and only those who are not indifferent to these goods can be persuaded that the study of philosophy is not a waste of time.

Philosophy, like all other studies, aims primarily at knowledge. The knowledge it aims at is the kind of knowledge which gives unity and system to the body of the sciences, and the kind which results from a critical examination of the grounds of our convictions, prejudices, and beliefs. But it cannot be maintained that philosophy has had any very great measure of success in its attempts to provide definite answers to its questions. If you ask a mathematician, a mineralogist, a historian, or any other man of learning, what definite body of truths has been ascertained by his science, his answer will last as long as you are willing to listen. But if you put the same question to a philosopher, he will, if he is candid, have to confess that his study has not achieved positive results such as have been achieved by other sciences. It is true that this is partly accounted for by the fact that, as soon as definite knowledge concerning any subject becomes possible, this subject ceases to be called philosophy, and becomes a separate science. The whole study of the heavens, which now belongs to astronomy, was once included in philosophy; Newton's great work was called "the mathematical principles of natural philosophy." Similarly, the study of the human mind, which was, until very lately, a part of philosophy, has now been separated from philosophy and has become the science of psychology. Thus, to a great extent, the uncertainty of philosophy is more apparent than real: those questions which are already capable of definite answers are placed in the sciences, while those only to which, at present, no definite answer can be given, remain to form the residue which is called philosophy.

This is, however, only a part of the truth concerning the uncertainty of philosophy. There are many questions—and among them those that are of the profoundest interest to our spiritual life—which, so far as we can see, must remain insoluble to the human intellect unless its powers become of quite a different order from what they are now. Has the universe any unity of plan or purpose, or is it a fortuitous concourse of atoms? Is consciousness a permanent part of the universe, giving hope of indefinite growth in wisdom, or is it a transitory accident on a small planet on which life must ultimately become impossible? Are good and evil of importance to the universe or only to man? Such questions are asked by philosophy, and variously answered by various philosophers. But it would seem that, whether answers be otherwise discoverable or not, the answers suggested by philosophy are none of them demonstrably true. Yet, however slight may be the hope of discovering an answer, it is part of the business of philosophy to continue the consideration of such questions, to make us aware of their importance, to examine all the approaches to them, and to keep alive that speculative interest in the universe which is apt to be killed by confining ourselves to definitely ascertainable knowledge.

Many philosophers, it is true, have held that philosophy could establish the truth of certain answers to such fundamental questions. They have supposed that what is of most importance in religious beliefs could be proved by strict demonstration to be true. In order to judge of such attempts, it is necessary to take a survey of human knowledge, and to form an opinion as to its methods and its limitations. On such a subject it would be unwise to pronounce dogmatically; but if the investigations of our previous chapters have not led us astray, we shall be compelled to renounce the hope of finding philosophical proofs of religious beliefs. We cannot, therefore, include as part of the value of philosophy any definite set of answers to such questions. Hence, once more, the value of philosophy must not depend upon any supposed body of definitely ascertainable knowledge to be acquired by those who study it.

The value of philosophy is, in fact, to be sought largely in its very uncertainty. The man who has no tincture of philosophy goes through life imprisoned in the prejudices derived from common sense, from the habitual beliefs of his age or his nation, and from convictions which have grown up in his mind without the co-operation or consent of his deliberate reason. To such a man the world tends to become definite, finite, obvious; common objects rouse no questions, and unfamiliar possibilities are contemptuously rejected. As soon as we begin to philosophise, on the contrary, we find, as we saw in our opening chapters, that even the most everyday things lead to problems to which only very incomplete answers can be given. Philosophy, though unable to tell us with certainty what is the true answer to the doubts which it raises, is able to suggest many possibilities which enlarge our thoughts and free them from the tyranny of custom. Thus, while diminishing our feeling of certainty as to what things are, it greatly increases our knowledge as to what they may be; it removes the somewhat arrogant dogmatism of those who have never travelled into the region of liberating doubt, and it keeps alive our sense of wonder by showing familiar things in an unfamiliar aspect.

Apart from its utility in showing unsuspected possibilities, philosophy has a value—perhaps its chief value—through the greatness of the objects which it contemplates, and the freedom from narrow and personal aims resulting from this contemplation. The life of the instinctive man is shut up within the circle of his private interests: family and friends may be included, but the outer world is not regarded except as it may help or hinder what comes within the circle of instinctive wishes. In such a life there is something feverish and confined, in comparison with which the philosophic life is calm and free. The private world of instinctive interests is a small one, set in the midst of a great and powerful world which must, sooner or later, lay our private world in ruins. Unless we can so enlarge our interests as to include the whole outer world, we remain like a garrison in a beleaguered fortress, knowing that the enemy prevents escape and that ultimate surrender is inevitable. In such a life there is no peace, but a constant strife between the insistence of desire and the powerlessness of will. In one way or another, if our life is to be great and free, we must escape this prison and this strife.

One way of escape is by philosophic contemplation. Philosophic contemplation does not, in its widest survey, divide the universe into two hostile camps—friends and foes, helpful and hostile, good and bad—it views the whole impartially. Philosophic contemplation, when it is unalloyed, does not aim at proving that the rest of the universe is akin to man. All acquisition of knowledge is an enlargement of the Self, but this enlargement is best attained when it is not directly sought. It is obtained when the desire for knowledge is alone operative, by a study which does not wish in advance that its objects should have this or that character, but adapts the Self to the characters which it finds in its objects. This enlargement of Self is not obtained when, taking the Self as it is, we try to show that the world is so similar to this Self that knowledge of it is possible without any admission of what seems alien. The desire to prove this is a form of self-assertion, and like all self-assertion, it is an obstacle to the growth of Self which it desires, and of which the Self knows that it is capable. Self-assertion, in philosophic speculation as elsewhere, views the world as a means to its own ends; thus it makes the world of less account than Self, and the Self sets bounds to the greatness of its goods. In contemplation, on the contrary, we start from the not-Self, and through its greatness the boundaries of Self are enlarged; through the infinity of the universe the mind which contemplates it achieves some share in infinity.

For this reason greatness of soul is not fostered by those philosophies which assimilate the universe to Man. Knowledge is a form of union of Self and not-Self; like all union, it is impaired by dominion, and therefore by any attempt to force the universe into conformity with what we find in ourselves. There is a widespread philosophical tendency towards the view which tells us that man is the measure of all things, that truth is man-made, that space and time and the world of universals are properties of the mind, and that, if there be anything not created by the mind, it is unknowable and of no account for us. This view, if our previous discussions were correct, is untrue; but in addition to being untrue, it has the effect of robbing philosophic contemplation of all that gives it value, since it fetters contemplation to Self. What it calls knowledge is not a union with the not-Self, but a set of prejudices, habits, and desires, making an impenetrable veil between us and the world beyond. The man who finds pleasure in such a theory of knowledge is like the man who never leaves the domestic circle for fear his word might not be law.

The true philosophic contemplation, on the contrary, finds its satisfaction in every enlargement of the not-Self, in everything that magnifies the objects contemplated, and thereby the subject contemplating. Everything, in contemplation, that is personal or private, everything that depends upon habit, self-interest, or desire, distorts the object, and hence impairs the union which the intellect seeks. By thus making a barrier between subject and object, such personal and private things become a prison to the intellect. The free intellect will see as God might see, without a *here* and *now*, without hopes and fears, without the trammels of customary beliefs and traditional prejudices, calmly, dispassionately, in the sole and exclusive desire of knowledge—knowledge as impersonal, as purely contemplative, as it is possible for man to attain. Hence also the free intellect will value more the abstract and universal knowledge into which the accidents of private history do not enter, than the knowledge brought by the senses, and dependent, as such knowledge must be, upon an exclusive and personal point of view and a body whose sense-organs distort as much as they reveal.

The mind which has become accustomed to the freedom and impartiality of philosophic contemplation will preserve something of the same freedom and impartiality in the world of action and emotion. It will view its purposes and desires as parts of the whole, with the absence of insistence that results from seeing them as infinitesimal fragments in a world of which all the rest is unaffected by any one man's deeds. The impartiality which, in contemplation, is the unalloyed desire for truth, is the very same quality of mind which, in action, is justice, and in emotion is that universal love which can be given to all, and not only to those who are judged useful or admirable. Thus contemplation enlarges not only the objects of our thoughts, but also the objects of our actions and our affections: it makes us citizens of the universe, not only of one walled city at war with all the rest. In this citizenship of the universe consists man's true freedom, and his liberation from the thraldom of narrow hopes and fears.

Thus, to sum up our discussion of the value of philosophy: Philosophy is to be studied, not for the sake of any definite answers to its questions, since no definite answers can, as a rule, be known to be true, but rather for the sake of the questions themselves; because these questions enlarge our conception of what is possible, enrich our intellectual imagination, and diminish the dogmatic assurance which closes the mind against speculation; but above all because, through the greatness of the universe which philosophy contemplates, the mind also is rendered great, and becomes capable of that union with the universe which constitutes its highest good.

BIBLIOGRAPHICAL NOTE

The student who wishes to acquire an elementary knowledge of philosophy will find it both easier and more profitable to read some of the works of the great philosophers than to attempt to derive an all-round view from hand-books. The following are specially recommended:

Plato: Republic, especially Books VI and VII. Translated by Davies and Vaughan. Golden Treasury Series.

Descartes: Meditations. Translated by Haldane and Ross. Cambridge University Press, 1911.

Spinoza: Ethics. Translated by Hale White and Amelia Stirling.

Leibniz: The Monadology. Translated by R. Latta. Oxford, 1898.

Berkeley: Three Dialogues between Hylas and Philonous.

Hume: Enquiry concerning Human Understanding.

Kant: Prolegomena to every Future Metaphysic.

INDEX

The interrogations indicate places where a view is discussed, not asserted.

THE HOME UNIVERSITY LIBRARY *of Modern Knowledge*

Is made up of absolutely new books by leading authorities.

The editors are *Professors Gilbert Murray, H. A. L. Fisher, W. T. Brewster, and J. Arthur Thomson.*

Cloth bound, good paper, clear type, 256 pages, per volume, bibliographies, indices, also maps or illustrations where needed. Each complete and sold separately. *Per volume.* **50 cents.**

LITERATURE AND ART.

[*Order Number*]

73. **EURIPIDES AND HIS AGE. By Gilbert Murray,** Regius Professor of Greek, Oxford.

101. **DANTE. By Jefferson B. Fletcher,** Columbia University. An interpretation of Dante and his teaching from his writings.

2. **SHAKESPEARE. By John Masefield.** "One of the very few indispensable adjuncts to a Shakespearean Library."—*Boston Transcript.*

81. **CHAUCER AND HIS TIMES. By Grace E. Hadow,** Lecturer Lady Margaret Hall, Oxford; Late Reader, Bryn Mawr.

97. **MILTON. By John Bailey.**

59. **DR. JOHNSON AND HIS CIRCLE. By John Bailey.** Johnson's life, character, works, and friendships are surveyed; and there is a notable vindication of the "Genius of Boswell."

83. **WILLIAM MORRIS: HIS WORK AND INFLUENCE. By A. Clutton Brock,** author of "Shelley: The Man and the Poet." William Morris believed that the artist should toil for love of his work rather than the gain of his employer, and so he turned from making works of art to remaking society.

75. **SHELLEY, GODWIN AND THEIR CIRCLE. By H. N. Brailsford.** The influence of the French Revolution on England.

70. **ANCIENT ART AND RITUAL.** By Jane E. Harrison, LL. D., D. Litt. "One of the 100 most important books of 1913."—*New York Times Review.*

45. **MEDIEVAL ENGLISH LITERATURE.** By W. P. Ker, Professor of English Literature, University College, London. "One of the soundest scholars. His style is effective, simple, yet never dry."—*The Athenaeum.*

87. **THE RENAISSANCE.** By Edith Sichel, author of "Catherine de Medici," "Men and Women of the French Renaissance."

89. **ELIZABETHAN LITERATURE.** By J. M. Robertson, M. P., author of "Montaigne and Shakespeare," "Modern Humanists."

27. **MODERN ENGLISH LITERATURE.** By G. H. Mair. From Wyatt and Surrey to Synge and Yeats. "One of the best of this great series."—*Chicago Evening Post.*

61. **THE VICTORIAN AGE IN LITERATURE.** By G. K. Chesterton.

40. **THE ENGLISH LANGUAGE.** By L. P. Smith. A concise history of its origin and development.

66. **WRITING ENGLISH PROSE.** By William T. Brewster, Professor of English, Columbia University. "Should be put into the hands of every man who is beginning to write and of every teacher of English that has brains enough to understand sense."—*New York Sun.*

58. **THE NEWSPAPER.** By G. Binney Dibble. The first full account from the inside of newspaper organization as it exists to-day.

48. **GREAT WRITERS OF AMERICA.** By W. P. Trent and John Erskine, Columbia University.

93. **AN OUTLINE OF RUSSIAN LITERATURE.** By Maurice Baring, author of "The Russian People," etc. Tolstoi, Tourgenieff, Dostoieffsky, Pushkin (the father of Russian Literature), Saltykov (the satirist,) Leskov, and many other authors.

31. **LANDMARKS IN FRENCH LITERATURE.** By G. L. Strachey, Scholar of Trinity College, Cambridge. "It is difficult to imagine how a better account of French Literature could be given in 250 pages."—*London Times.*

64. **THE LITERATURE OF GERMANY.** By J. G. Robertson.

62. **PAINTERS AND PAINTING.** By Sir Frederick Wedmore. With 16 half-tone illustrations.

38. **ARCHITECTURE.** By Prof. W. R. Lethaby. An introduction to the history and theory of the art of building.

NATURAL SCIENCE.

68. **DISEASE AND ITS CAUSES.** By W. T. Councilman, M. D., LL. D., Professor of Pathology, Harvard University.

85. **SEX.** By J. Arthur Thompson and Patrick Geddes, joint authors of "The Evolution of Sex."

71. **PLANT LIFE.** By J. B. Farmer, D. Sc., F. R. S., Professor of Botany in the Imperial College of Science, London. This very fully illustrated volume contains an account of the salient features of plant form and function.

63. **THE ORIGIN AND NATURE OF LIFE.** By Benjamin M. Moore, Professor of Bio-Chemistry, Liverpool.

90. **CHEMISTRY.** By Raphael Meldola, F. R. S., Professor of Chemistry, Finsbury Technical College. Presents the way in which the science has developed and the stage it has reached.

53. **ELECTRICITY.** By Gisbert Kapp, Professor of Electrical Engineering, University of Birmingham.

54. **THE MAKING OF THE EARTH.** By J. W. Gregory, Professor of Geology, Glasgow University. 38 maps and figures. Describes the origin of the earth, the formation and changes of its surface and structure, its geological history, the first appearance of life, and its influence upon the globe.

56. **MAN: A HISTORY OF THE HUMAN BODY.** By A. Keith, M. D., Hunterian Professor, Royal College of Surgeons, London. Shows how the human body developed.

74. **NERVES.** By David Fraser Harris, M. D., Professor of Physiology, Dalhousie University, Halifax. Explains in non-technical language the place and powers of the nervous system.

21. **AN INTRODUCTION TO SCIENCE.** By Prof. J. Arthur Thomson, Science Editor of the Home University Library. For those unacquainted with the scientific volumes in the series, this would prove an excellent introduction.

14. **EVOLUTION.** By Prof. J. Arthur Thomson and Prof. Patrick Geddes. Explains to the layman what the title means to the scientific world.

23. **ASTRONOMY.** By A. R. Hinks, Chief Assistant at the Cambridge Observatory. "Decidedly original in substance, and the most readable and informative little book on modern astronomy we have seen for a long time."—*Nature*.

24. **PSYCHICAL RESEARCH.** By Prof. W. F. Barrett, formerly President of the Society for Psychical Research.

9. **THE EVOLUTION OF PLANTS.** By Dr. D. H. Scott, President of the Linnean Society of London. The story of the development of flowering plants, from the earliest zoological times, unlocked from technical language.

43. **MATTER AND ENERGY.** By F. Soddy, Lecturer in Physical Chemistry and Radioactivity, University of Glasgow. "Brilliant. Can hardly be surpassed. Sure to attract attention."—*New York Sun.*

41. **PSYCHOLOGY, THE STUDY OF BEHAVIOUR.** By William McDougall, of Oxford. A well digested summary of the essentials of the science put in excellent literary form by a leading authority.

42. **THE PRINCIPLES OF PHYSIOLOGY.** By Prof. J. G. McKendrick. A compact statement by the Emeritus Professor at Glasgow, for uninstructed readers.

37. **ANTHROPOLOGY.** By R. R. Marett, Reader in Social Anthropology, Oxford. Seeks to plot out and sum up the general series of changes, bodily and mental, undergone by man in the course of history. "Excellent. So enthusiastic, so clear and witty, and so well adapted to the general reader."—*American Library Association Booklist.*

17. **CRIME AND INSANITY.** By Dr. C. Mercier, author of "Test Book of Insanity," etc.

12. **THE ANIMAL WORLD.** By Prof. F. W. Gamble.

15. **INTRODUCTION TO MATHEMATICS.** By A. N. Whitehead, author of "Universal Algebra."

PHILOSOPHY AND RELIGION.

69. **A HISTORY OF FREEDOM OF THOUGHT.** By John B. Bury, M. A., LL. D., Regius Professor of Modern History in Cambridge University. Summarizes the history of the long struggle between authority and reason and of the emergence of the principle that coercion of opinion is a mistake.

96. **A HISTORY OF PHILOSOPHY.** By Clement C. J. Webb, Oxford.

35. **THE PROBLEMS OF PHILOSOPHY.** By Bertrand Russell, Lecturer and Late Fellow, Trinity College, Cambridge.

60. **COMPARATIVE RELIGION.** By Prof. J. Estlin Carpenter. "One of the few authorities on this subject compares all the religions to see what they have to offer on the great themes of religion."—*Christian Work and Evangelist.*

44. **BUDDHISM.** By Mrs. Rhys Davids, Lecturer on Indian Philosophy, Manchester.

46. **ENGLISH SECTS: A HISTORY OF NONCONFORMITY.** By W. B. Selbie, Principal of Manchester College, Oxford.

55. **MISSIONS: THEIR RISE AND DEVELOPMENT. By Mrs. Mandell Creighton,** author of "History of England." The author seeks to prove that missions have done more to civilize the world than any other human agency.

52. **ETHICS. By G. E. Moore,** Lecturer in Moral Science, Cambridge. Discusses what is right and what is wrong, and the whys and wherefores.

65. **THE LITERATURE OF THE OLD TESTAMENT. By George F. Moore,** Professor of the History of Religion, Harvard University. "A popular work of the highest order. Will be profitable to anybody who cares enough about Bible study to read a serious book on the subject."—*American Journal of Theology.*

88. **RELIGIOUS DEVELOPMENT BETWEEN OLD AND NEW TESTAMENTS. By R. H. Charles,** Canon of Westminster. Shows how religious and ethical thought between 180 B. C. and 100 A. D. grew naturally into that of the New Testament.

50. **THE MAKING OF THE NEW TESTAMENT. By B. W. Bacon,** Professor of New Testament Criticism, Yale. An authoritative summary of the results of modern critical research with regard to the origins of the New Testament.

SOCIAL SCIENCE.

91. **THE NEGRO. By W. E. Burghardt DuBois,** author of "Souls of Black Folks," etc. A history of the black man in Africa, America or wherever else his presence has been or is important.

77. **CO-PARTNERSHIP AND PROFIT SHARING. By Aneurin Williams,** Chairman, Executive Committee, International Co-operative Alliance, etc. Explains the various types of co-partnership or profit-sharing, or both, and gives details of the arrangements now in force in many of the great industries.

99. **POLITICAL THOUGHT: THE UTILITARIANS. FROM BENTHAM TO J. S. MILL. By William L. P. Davidson.**

98. **POLITICAL THOUGHT: FROM HERBERT SPENCER TO THE PRESENT DAY. By Ernest Barker, M. A.**

79. **UNEMPLOYMENT. By A. C. Pigou, M. A.,** Professor of Political Economy at Cambridge. The meaning, measurement, distribution, and effects of unemployment, its relation to wages, trade fluctuations, and disputes, and some proposals of remedy or relief

80. **COMMON-SENSE IN LAW. By Prof. Paul Vinogradoff, D. C. L., LL. D.** Social and Legal Rules—Legal Rights and Duties—Facts and Acts in Law—Legislation—Custom—Judicial Precedents—Equity—The Law of Nature.

49. **ELEMENTS OF POLITICAL ECONOMY. By S. J. Chapman,** Professor of Political Economy and Dean of Faculty of Commerce and Administration, University of Manchester.

11. **THE SCIENCE OF WEALTH. By J. A. Hobson,** author of "Problems of Poverty." A study of the structure and working of the modern business world.

1. **PARLIAMENT. ITS HISTORY, CONSTITUTION, AND PRACTICE. By Sir Courtenay P. Ilbert,** Clerk of the House of Commons.

16. **LIBERALISM. By Prof. L. T. Hobhouse,** author of "Democracy and Reaction." A masterly philosophical and historical review of the subject.

5. **THE STOCK EXCHANGE. By F. W. Hirst,** Editor of the London *Economist.* Reveals to the non-financial mind the facts about investment, speculation, and the other terms which the title suggests.

10. **THE SOCIALIST MOVEMENT. By J. Ramsay Macdonald,** Chairman of the British Labor Party.

28. **THE EVOLUTION OF INDUSTRY. By D. H. MacGregor,** Professor of Political Economy, University of Leeds. An outline of the recent changes that have given us the present conditions of the working classes and the principles involved.

29. **ELEMENTS OF ENGLISH LAW. By W. M. Geldart,** Vinerian Professor of English Law, Oxford. A simple statement of the basic principles of the English legal system on which that of the United States is based.

32. **THE SCHOOL: AN INTRODUCTION TO THE STUDY OF EDUCATION. By J. J. Findlay,** Professor of Education, Manchester. Presents the history, the psychological basis, and the theory of the school with a rare power of summary and suggestion.

6. **IRISH NATIONALITY. By Mrs. J. R. Green.** A brilliant account of the genius and mission of the Irish people. "An entrancing work, and I would advise every one with a drop of Irish blood in his veins or a vein of Irish sympathy in his heart to read it."—*New York Times' Review.*

GENERAL HISTORY AND GEOGRAPHY.

33. **THE HISTORY OF ENGLAND. By A. F. Pollard,** Professor of English History, University of London.

95. **BELGIUM. By R. C. K. Ensor,** Sometime Scholar of Balliol College. The geographical, linguistic, historical, artistic and literary associations.

100. **POLAND. By W. Alison Phillips,** University of Dublin. The history of Poland with special emphasis upon the Polish question of the present day.

34. **CANADA. By A. G. Bradley.**

72. **GERMANY OF TO-DAY. By Charles Tower.**

78. **LATIN AMERICA. By William R. Shepherd,** Professor of History, Columbia. With maps. The historical, artistic, and commercial development of the Central South American republics.

18. **THE OPENING-UP OF AFRICA. By Sir H. H. Johnston.** The first living authority on the subject tells how and why the "native races" went to the various parts of Africa and summarizes its exploration and colonization.

19. **THE CIVILIZATION OF CHINA. By H. A. Giles,** Professor of Chinese, Cambridge.

36. **PEOPLES AND PROBLEMS OF INDIA. By Sir T. W. Holderness.** "The best small treatise dealing with the range of subjects fairly indicated by the title."—*The Dial.*

26. **THE DAWN OF HISTORY. By J. L. Myers,** Professor of Ancient History, Oxford.

92. **THE ANCIENT EAST. By D. G. Hogarth, M. A., F. B. A., F. S. A.** Connects with Prof. Myers's "Dawn of History" (No. 26) at about 1000 B. C. and reviews the history of Assyria, Babylon, Cilicia, Persia and Macedon.

30. **ROME. By W. Warde Fowler,** author of "Social Life at Rome," etc. "A masterly sketch of Roman character and what it did for the world."—*London Spectator.*

13. **MEDIEVAL EUROPE. By H. W. C. Davis,** Fellow at Balliol College, Oxford, author of "Charlemagne," etc.

3. **THE FRENCH REVOLUTION. By Hillaire Belloc.**

57. **NAPOLEON. By H. A. L. Fisher,** Vice-Chancellor of Sheffield University. Author of "The Republican Tradition in Europe."

20. **HISTORY OF OUR TIME (1885-1911). By C. P. Gooch,** A "moving picture" of the world since 1885.

22. **THE PAPACY AND MODERN TIMES. By Rev. William Barry, D. D.,** author of "The Papal Monarchy," etc. The story of the rise and fall of the Temporal Power.

4. **A SHORT HISTORY OF WAR AND PEACE.** By **G. H. Perris**, author of "Russia in Revolution," etc.

94. **THE NAVY AND SEA POWER.** By **David Hannay**, author of "Short History of the Royal Navy," etc. A brief history of the navies, sea power, and ship growth of all nations, including the rise and decline of America on the sea, and explaining the present British supremacy thereon.

8. **POLAR EXPLORATION.** By **Dr. W. S. Bruce**, Leader of the "Scotia" expedition. Emphasizes the results of the expeditions.

51. **MASTER MARINERS.** By **John R. Spears**, author of "The History of Our Navy," etc. A history of sea craft adventure from the earliest times.

86. **EXPLORATION OF THE ALPS.** By **Arnold Lunn, M. A.**

7. **MODERN GEOGRAPHY.** By **Dr. Marion Newbigin**. Shows the relation of physical features to living things and to some of the chief institutions of civilization.

76. **THE OCEAN. A GENERAL ACCOUNT OF THE SCIENCE OF THE SEA.** By **Sir John Murray, K. C. B.**, Naturalist H. M. S. "Challenger," 1872-1876, joint author of "The Depths of the Ocean," etc.

84. **THE GROWTH OF EUROPE.** By **Granville Cole**, Professor of Geology, Royal College of Science, Ireland. A study of the geology and physical geography in connection with the political geography.

AMERICAN HISTORY.

47. **THE COLONIAL PERIOD (1607-1766).** By **Charles McLean Andrews**, Professor of American History, Yale.

82. **THE WARS BETWEEN ENGLAND AND AMERICA (1763-1815).** By **Theodore C. Smith**, Professor of American History, Williams College. A history of the period, with especial emphasis on The Revolution and The War of 1812.

67. **FROM JEFFERSON TO LINCOLN (1815-1860).** By **William MacDonald**, Professor of History, Brown University. The author makes the history of this period circulate about constitutional ideas and slavery sentiment.

25. **THE CIVIL WAR (1854-1865.)** By **Frederic L. Paxson**, Professor of American History, University of Wisconsin.

39. **RECONSTRUCTION AND UNION (1865-1912).** By **Paul Leland Haworth**. A History of the United States in our own times.

OTHER VOLUMES IN PREPARATION

HENRY HOLT AND COMPANY

34 West 33d Street New York

www.ingramcontent.com/pod-product-compliance
Ingram Content Group UK Ltd.
Pitfield, Milton Keynes, MK11 3LW, UK
UKHW040657061026
15647UKWH00012B/37/J

9 789351 286134